Modern Mythology

Andrew Lang

Modern Mythology

ISBN: 978-1-64799-556-0

DEDICATION

Dedicated to the memory of John Fergus McLennan

CONTENTS

INTRODUCTION

It may well be doubted whether works of controversy serve any useful purpose. 'On an opponent,' as Mr. Matthew Arnold said, 'one never does make any impression,' though one may hope that controversy sometimes illuminates a topic in the eyes of impartial readers. The pages which follow cannot but seem wandering and desultory, for they are a reply to a book, Mr. Max Müller's Contributions to the Science of Mythology, in which the attack is of a skirmishing character. Throughout more than eight hundred pages the learned author keeps up an irregular fire at the ideas and methods of the anthropological school of mythologists. The reply must follow the lines of attack.

Criticism cannot dictate to an author how he shall write his own book. Yet anthropologists and folk-lorists, 'agriologists' and 'Hottentotic' students, must regret that Mr. Max Müller did not state their general theory, as he understands it, fully and once for all. Adversaries rarely succeed in quite understanding each other; but had Mr. Max Müller made such a statement, we could have cleared up anything in our position which might seem to him obscure.

Our system is but one aspect of the theory of evolution, or is but the application of that theory to the topic of mythology. The archæologist studies human life in its material remains; he tracks progress (and occasional degeneration) from the rudely chipped flints in the ancient gravel beds, to the polished stone weapon, and thence to the ages of bronze and iron. He is guided by material 'survivals'—ancient arms, implements, and ornaments. The student of Institutions has a similar method. He finds his relics of the uncivilised past in agricultural usages, in archaic methods of allotment of land, in odd marriage customs, things rudimentary— fossil relics, as it were, of an early social and political condition. The archæologist and the student of Institutions compare these relics, material or customary, with the weapons, pottery, implements, or again with the habitual law and usage of existing savage or barbaric races, and demonstrate that our weapons and tools, and our laws and manners, have been slowly evolved out of lower conditions, even out of savage conditions.

The anthropological method in mythology is the same. In civilised religion and myth we find rudimentary survivals, fossils of rite and creed, ideas absolutely incongruous with the environing morality, philosophy, and science of Greece and India. Parallels to these things, so out of keeping with civilisation, we recognise in the creeds and rites of the lower races, even of cannibals; but there the creeds and rites are not incongruous with their environment of knowledge and culture. There they are as natural and inevitable as the flint-headed spear or marriage by capture. We argue, therefore, that religions and mythical faiths and rituals which, among Greeks and Indians, are inexplicably incongruous have lived on from an age in which they were natural and inevitable, an age of savagery.

That is our general position, and it would have been a benefit to us if Mr. Max Müller had stated it in his own luminous way, if he wished to oppose us, and had shown us where and how it fails to meet the requirements of scientific method. In place of doing this once for all, he often assails our evidence, yet never notices the defences of our evidence, which our school has been offering for over a hundred years. He attacks the excesses of which some sweet anthropological enthusiasts have been guilty or may be guilty, such as seeing totems wherever they find beasts in ancient religion, myth, or art. He asks for definitions (as of totemism), but never, I think, alludes to the authoritative definitions by Mr. McLennan and Mr. Frazer. He assails the theory of fetishism as if it stood now where De Brosses left it in a purely pioneer work—or, rather, where he understands De Brosses to have left it. One might as well attack the atomic theory where Lucretius left it, or the theory of evolution where it was left by the elder Darwin.

Thus Mr. Max Müller really never conies to grips with his opponents, and his large volumes shine rather in erudition and style than in method and system. Anyone who attempts a reply must necessarily follow Mr. Max Müller up and down, collecting his scattered remarks on this or that point at issue. Hence my reply, much against my will, must seem desultory and rambling. But I have endeavoured to answer with some kind of method and system, and I even hope that this little book may be useful as a kind of supplement to Mr. Max Müller's, for it contains exact references to certain works of which he takes the reader's knowledge for granted.

The general problem at issue is apt to be lost sight of in this guerilla kind of warfare. It is perhaps more distinctly stated in the preface to Mr. Max Müller's Chips from a German Workshop, vol. iv. (Longmans, 1895), than in his two recent volumes. The general problem is this: Has language—especially language in a state of 'disease,' been the great source of the mythology of the world? Or does mythology, on the whole, represent the survival of an old stage of thought—not caused by language—from which civilised men have slowly emancipated themselves? Mr. Max Müller is of the former, anthropologists are of the latter, opinion. Both, of course, agree that myths are a product of thought, of a kind of thought almost extinct in civilised races; but Mr. Max Müller holds that language caused that kind of thought. We, on the other hand, think that language only gave it one means of expressing itself.

The essence of myth, as of fairy tale, we agree, is the conception of the things in the world as all alike animated, personal, capable of endless interchanges of form. Men may become beasts; beasts may change into men; gods may appear as human or bestial; stones, plants, winds, water, may speak and act like human beings, and change shapes with them.

Anthropologists demonstrate that the belief in this universal kinship, universal personality of things, which we find surviving only in the myths of civilised races, is even now to some degree part of the living creed of savages. Civilised myths, then, they urge, are survivals from a parallel state of belief once prevalent among the ancestors of even the Aryan race. But how did this mental condition, this early sort of false metaphysics, come into existence? We have no direct historical information on the subject. If I were obliged to offer an hypothesis, it would be that early men, conscious of personality, will, and life—conscious that force, when exerted by themselves, followed on a determination of will within them—extended that explanation to all the exhibitions of force which they beheld without them. Rivers run (early man thought), winds blow, fire burns, trees wave, as a result of their own will, the will of personal conscious entities. Such vitality, and even power of motion, early man attributed even to inorganic matter, as rocks and stones. All these things were beings, like man himself. This does not appear to me an unnatural kind of nascent, half-conscious metaphysics. 'Man never knows how much he anthropomorphises.' He extended the only explanation of his own action which consciousness yielded to him, he extended it to explain every other sort of action in the sensible world. Early Greek philosophy recognised the stars as living bodies; all things had once seemed living and personal. From the beginning, man was eager causas cognoscere rerum. The only cause about which self-consciousness gave him any knowledge was his own personal will. He therefore supposed all things to be animated with a like will and personality. His mythology is a philosophy of things, stated in stories based on the belief in universal personality.

My theory of the origin of that belief is, of course, a mere guess; we have never seen any race in the process of passing from a total lack of a hypothesis of causes into that hypothesis of universally distributed personality which is the basis of mythology.

But Mr. Max Müller conceives that this belief in universally distributed personality (the word 'Animism' is not very clear) was the result of an historical necessity—not of speculation, but of language. 'Roots were all, or nearly all, expressive of action. . . . Hence a river could only be called or conceived as a runner, or a roarer, or a defender; and in all these capacities always as something active and animated, nay, as something masculine or feminine.'

But why conceived as 'masculine or feminine'? This necessity for endowing inanimate though active things, such as rivers, with sex, is obviously a necessity of a stage of thought wholly unlike our own. We know that active inanimate things are sexless, are neuter; we feel no necessity to speak of them as male or female. How did the first speakers of the human race come to be obliged to call lifeless things by names connoting sex, and therefore connoting, not only activity, but also life and personality? We explain it by the theory that man called lifeless things male or female—by using gender-terminations—as a result of his habit of regarding lifeless things as personal beings; that habit, again, being the result of his consciousness of himself as a living will.

Mr. Max Müller takes the opposite view. Man did not call lifeless things by names denoting sex because he regarded them as persons; he came to regard them as persons because he had already given them names connoting sex. And why had he done that? This is what Mr. Max Müller does not explain. He says:

'In ancient languages every one of these words' (sky, earth, sea, rain) 'had necessarily' (why necessarily?) 'a termination expressive of gender, and this naturally produced in the mind the corresponding idea of sex, so that these names received not only an individual but a sexual character.'[1]

It is curious that, in proof apparently of this, Mr. Max Müller cites a passage from the Printer's Register, in which we read that to little children 'everything is alive. . . . The same instinct that prompts the child to personify everything remains unchecked in the savage, and grows up with him to manhood. Hence in all simple and early languages there are but two genders, masculine and feminine.'

The Printer's Register states our theory in its own words. First came the childlike and savage belief in universal personality. Thence arose the genders, masculine and feminine, in early languages. These ideas are the precise reverse of Mr. Max Müller's ideas. In his opinion, genders in language caused the belief in the universal personality even of inanimate things. The Printer's Register holds that the belief in universal personality, on the other

---

[1] Chips, iv. 62.

hand, caused the genders. Yet for thirty years, since 1868, Mr. Max Müller has been citing his direct adversary, in the Printer's Register, as a supporter of his opinion! We, then, hold that man thought all things animated, and expressed his belief in gender-terminations. Mr. Max Müller holds that, because man used gender-terminations, therefore he thought all things animated, and so he became mythopœic. In the passage cited, Mr. Max Müller does not say why 'in ancient languages every one of these words had necessarily terminations expressive of gender.' He merely quotes the hypothesis of the Printer's Register. If he accepts that hypothesis, it destroys his own theory—that gender-terminations caused all things to be regarded as personal; for, ex hypothesi, it was just because they were regarded as personal that they received names with gender-terminations. Somewhere—I cannot find the reference—Mr. Max Müller seems to admit that personalising thought caused gender-terminations, but these later 'reacted' on thought, an hypothesis which multiplies causes præter necessitatem.

Here, then, at the very threshold of the science of mythology we find Mr. Max Müller at once maintaining that a feature of language, gender-terminations, caused the mythopœic state of thought, and quoting with approval the statement that the mythopœic state of thought caused gender-terminations.

Mr. Max Müller's whole system of mythology is based on reasoning analogous to this example. His mot d'ordre, as Professor Tiele says, is 'a disease of language.' This theory implies universal human degradation. Man was once, for all we know, rational enough; but his mysterious habit of using gender-terminations, and his perpetual misconceptions of the meaning of old words in his own language, reduced him to the irrational and often (as we now say) obscene and revolting absurdities of his myths. Here (as is later pointed out) the objection arises, that all languages must have taken the disease in the same way. A Maori myth is very like a Greek myth. If the Greek myth arose from a disease of Greek, how did the wholly different Maori speech, and a score of others, come to have precisely the same malady?

Mr. Max Müller alludes to a Maori parallel to the myth of Cronos.[2] 'We can only say that there is a rusty lock in New Zealand, and a rusty lock in Greece, and that, surely, is very small comfort.' He does not take the point. The point is that, as the myth occurs in two remote and absolutely unconnected languages, a theory of disease of language cannot turn the wards of the rusty locks. The myth is, in part at least, a nature-myth—an attempt to account for

[2] Chips, iv. p. xxxv.

the severance of Heaven and Earth (once united) by telling a story in which natural phenomena are animated and personal. A disease of language has nothing to do with this myth. It is cited as a proof against the theory of disease of language.

The truth is, that while languages differ, men (and above all early men) have the same kind of thoughts, desires, fancies, habits, institutions. It is not that in which all races formally differ—their language—but that in which all early races are astonishingly the same—their ideas, fancies, habits, desires—that causes the amazing similarity of their myths.

Mythologists, then, who find in early human nature the living ideas which express themselves in myths will hardily venture to compare the analogous myths of all peoples. Mythologists, on the other hand, who find the origin of myths in a necessity imposed upon thought by misunderstood language will necessarily, and logically, compare only myths current among races who speak languages of the same family. Thus, throughout Mr. Max Müller's new book we constantly find him protesting, on the whole and as a rule, against the system which illustrates Aryan myths by savage parallels. Thus he maintains that it is perilous to make comparative use of myths current in languages—say, Maori or Samoyed—which the mythologists confessedly do not know. To this we can only reply that we use the works of the best accessible authorities, men who do know the languages—say, Dr. Codrington or Bishop Callaway, or Castren or Egede. Now it is not maintained that the myths, on the whole, are incorrectly translated. The danger which we incur, it seems, is ignorance of the original sense of savage or barbaric divine or heroic names—say, Maui, or Yehl, or Huitzilopochhtli, or Heitsi Eibib, or Pundjel. By Mr. Max Müller's system such names are old words, of meanings long ago generally lost by the speakers of each language, but analysable by 'true scholars' into their original significance. That will usually be found by the philologists to indicate 'the inevitable Dawn,' or Sun, or Night, or the like, according to the taste and fancy of the student.

To all this a reply is urged in the following pages. In agreement with Curtius and many other scholars, we very sincerely doubt almost all etymologies of old proper names, even in Greek or Sanskrit. We find among philologists, as a rule, the widest discrepancies of interpretation. Moreover, every name must mean something. Now, whatever the meaning of a name (supposing it to be really ascertained), very little ingenuity is needed to make it indicate one or other aspect of Dawn or Night, of Lightning or Storm, just as the philologist pleases. Then he explains the divine or heroic being denoted by the name—as Dawn or Storm, or Fire or

Night, or Twilight or Wind—in accordance with his private taste, easily accommodating the facts of the myth, whatever they may be, to his favourite solution. We rebel against this kind of logic, and persist in studying the myth in itself and in comparison with analogous myths in every accessible language. Certainly, if divine and heroic names—Artemis or Pundjel—can be interpreted, so much is gained. But the myth may be older than the name.

As Mr. Hogarth points out, Alexander has inherited in the remote East the myths of early legendary heroes. We cannot explain these by the analysis of the name of Alexander! Even if the heroic or divine name can be shown to be the original one (which is practically impossible), the meaning of the name helps us little. That Zeus means 'sky' cannot conceivably explain scores of details in the very composite legend of Zeus—say, the story of Zeus, Demeter, and the Ram. Moreover, we decline to admit that, if a divine name means 'swift,' its bearer must be the wind or the sunlight. Nor, if the name means 'white,' is it necessarily a synonym of Dawn, or of Lightning, or of Clear Air, or what not. But a mythologist who makes language and names the fountain of myth will go on insisting that myths can only be studied by people who know the language in which they are told. Mythologists who believe that human nature is the source of myths will go on comparing all myths that are accessible in translations by competent collectors.

Mr. Max Müller says, 'We seldom find mythology, as it were, in situ—as it lived in the minds and unrestrained utterances of the people. We generally have to study it in the works of mythographers, or in the poems of later generations, when it had long ceased to be living and intelligible.' The myths of Greece and Rome, in Hyginus or Ovid, 'are likely to be as misleading as a hortus siccus would be to a botanist if debarred from his rambles through meadows and hedges.'[3]

Nothing can be more true, or more admirably stated. These remarks are, indeed, the charter, so to speak, of anthropological mythology and of folklore. The old mythologists worked at a hortus siccus, at myths dried and pressed in thoroughly literary books, Greek and Latin. But we now study myths 'in the unrestrained utterances of the people,' either of savage tribes or of the European Folk, the unprogressive peasant class. The former, and to some extent the latter, still live in the mythopœic state of mind—regarding bees, for instance, as persons who must be told of a death in the family. Their myths are still not wholly out of concord with their habitual view of a world in which an old woman may become a

---

[3] Chips, iv. pp. vi. vii.

hare. As soon as learned Jesuits like Père Lafitau began to understand their savage flocks, they said, 'These men are living in Ovid's Metamorphoses.' They found mythology in situ! Hence mythologists now study mythology in situ—in savages and in peasants, who till very recently were still in the mythopœic stage of thought. Mannhardt made this idea his basis. Mr. Max Müller says,[4] very naturally, that I have been 'popularising the often difficult and complicated labours of Mannhardt and others.' In fact (as is said later), I published all my general conclusions before I had read Mannhardt. Quite independently I could not help seeing that among savages and peasants we had mythology, not in a literary hortus siccus, but in situ. Mannhardt, though he appreciated Dr. Tylor, had made, I think, but few original researches among savage myths and customs. His province was European folklore. What he missed will be indicated in the chapter on 'The Fire-Walk'—one example among many.

But this kind of mythology in situ, in 'the unrestrained utterances of the people,' Mr. Max Müller tells us, is no province of his. 'I saw it was hopeless for me to gain a knowledge at first hand of innumerable local legends and customs;' and it is to be supposed that he distrusted knowledge acquired by collectors: Grimm, Mannhardt, Campbell of Islay, and an army of others. 'A scholarlike knowledge of Maori or Hottentot mythology' was also beyond him. We, on the contrary, take our Maori lore from a host of collectors: Taylor, White, Manning ('The Pakeha Maori'), Tregear, Polack, and many others. From them we flatter ourselves that we get—as from Grimm, Mannhardt, Islay, and the rest—mythology in situ. We compare it with the dry mythologic blossoms of the classical hortus siccus, and with Greek ritual and temple legend, and with Märchen in the scholiasts, and we think the comparisons very illuminating. They have thrown new light on Greek mythology, ritual, mysteries, and religion. This much we think we have already done, though we do not know Maori, and though each of us can hope to gather but few facts from the mouths of living peasants.

Examples of the results of our method will be found in the following pages. Thus, if the myth of the fire-stealer in Greece is explained by misunderstood Greek or Sanskrit words in no way connected with robbery, we shall show that the myth of the theft of fire occurs where no Greek or Sanskrit words were ever spoken. There, we shall show, the myth arose from simple inevitable human ideas. We shall therefore doubt whether in Greece a common human myth had a singular cause—in a 'disease of language.'

---

[4] Ibid. iv. p. xv.

It is with no enthusiasm that I take the opportunity of Mr. Max Müller's reply to me 'by name.' Since Myth, Ritual, and Religion (now out of print, but accessible in the French of M. Marillier) was published, ten years ago, I have left mythology alone. The general method there adopted has been applied in a much more erudite work by Mr. Frazer, The Golden Bough, by Mr. Farnell in Cults of the Greek States, by Mr. Jevons in his Introduction to the History of Religion, by Miss Harrison in explanations of Greek ritual, by Mr. Hartland in The Legend of Perseus, and doubtless by many other writers. How much they excel me in erudition may be seen by comparing Mr. Farnell's passage on the Bear Artemis[5] with the section on her in this volume.

Mr. Max Müller observes that 'Mannhardt's mythological researches have never been fashionable.' They are now very much in fashion; they greatly inspire Mr. Frazer and Mr. Farnell. 'They seemed to me, and still seem to me, too exclusive,' says Mr. Max Müller.[6] Mannhardt in his second period was indeed chiefly concerned with myths connected, as he held, with agriculture and with tree-worship. Mr. Max Müller, too, has been thought 'exclusive'—'as teaching,' he complains, 'that the whole of mythology is solar.' That reproach arose, he says, because 'some of my earliest contributions to comparative mythology were devoted exclusively to the special subject of solar myths.'[7] But Mr. Max Müller also mentions his own complaints, of 'the omnipresent sun and the inevitable dawn appearing in ever so many disguises.'

Did they really appear? Were the myths, say the myths of Daphne, really solar? That is precisely what we hesitate to accept. In the same way Mannhardt's preoccupation with vegetable myths has tended, I think, to make many of his followers ascribe vegetable origins to myths and gods, where the real origin is perhaps for ever lost. The corn-spirit starts up in most unexpected places. Mr. Frazer, Mannhardt's disciple, is very severe on solar theories of Osiris, and connects that god with the corn-spirit. But Mannhardt did not go so far. Mannhardt thought that the myth of Osiris was solar. To my thinking, these resolutions of myths into this or that original source—solar, nocturnal, vegetable, or what not—are often very perilous. A myth so extremely composite as that of Osiris must be a stream flowing from many springs, and, as in the case of certain rivers, it is difficult or impossible to say which is the real fountain-head.

---

[5] Cults of the Greek States, ii. 435-440.
[6] Chips, iv. p. xiv.
[7] Chips, iv. p. xiii.

One would respectfully recommend to young mythologists great reserve in their hypotheses of origins. All this, of course, is the familiar thought of writers like Mr. Frazer and Mr. Farnell, but a tendency to seek for exclusively vegetable origins of gods is to be observed in some of the most recent speculations. I well know that I myself am apt to press a theory of totems too far, and in the following pages I suggest reserves, limitations, and alternative hypotheses. Il y a serpent et serpent; a snake tribe may be a local tribe named from the Snake River, not a totem kindred. The history of mythology is the history of rash, premature, and exclusive theories. We are only beginning to learn caution. Even the prevalent anthropological theory of the ghost-origin of religion might, I think, be advanced with caution (as Mr. Jevons argues on other grounds) till we know a little more about ghosts and a great deal more about psychology. We are too apt to argue as if the psychical condition of the earliest men were exactly like our own; while we are just beginning to learn, from Prof. William James, that about even our own psychical condition we are only now realising our exhaustive ignorance. How often we men have thought certain problems settled for good! How often we have been compelled humbly to return to our studies! Philological comparative mythology seemed securely seated for a generation. Her throne is tottering:

> *Our little systems have their day,*
> *They have their day and cease to be,*
> *They are but broken lights from Thee,*
> *And Thou, we trust, art more than they.*

But we need not hate each other for the sake of our little systems, like the grammarian who damned his rival's soul for his 'theory of the irregular verbs.' Nothing, I hope, is said here inconsistent with the highest esteem for Mr. Max Müller's vast erudition, his enviable style, his unequalled contributions to scholarship, and his awakening of that interest in mythological science without which his adversaries would probably never have existed.

Most of Chapter XII. appeared in the 'Contemporary Review,' and most of Chapter XIII. in the 'Princeton Review.'

REGENT MYTHOLOGY

Mythology in 1860-1880

Between 1860 and 1880, roughly speaking, English people interested in early myths and religions found the mythological theories of Professor Max Müller in possession of the field. These brilliant and attractive theories, taking them in the widest sense, were not, of course, peculiar to the Right Hon. Professor. In France, in Germany, in America, in Italy, many scholars agreed in his opinion that the science of language is the most potent spell for opening the secret chamber of mythology. But while these scholars worked on the same general principle as Mr. Max Müller, while they subjected the names of mythical beings—Zeus, Helen, Achilles, Athênê—to philological analysis, and then explained the stories of gods and heroes by their interpretations of the meanings of their names, they arrived at all sorts of discordant results. Where Mr. Max Müller found a myth of the Sun or of the Dawn, these scholars were apt to see a myth of the wind, of the lightning, of the thunder-cloud, of the crépuscule, of the upper air, of what each of them pleased. But these ideas—the ideas of Kuhn, Welcker, Curtius (when he appeared in the discussion), of Schwartz, of Lauer, of Bréal, of many others—were very little known—if known at all—to the English public. Captivated by the graces of Mr. Max Müller's manner, and by a style so pellucid that it accredited a logic perhaps not so clear, the public hardly knew of the divisions in the philological camp. They were unaware that, as Mannhardt says, the philological school had won 'few sure gains,' and had discredited their method by a 'muster-roll of variegated' and discrepant 'hypotheses.'

Now, in all sciences there are differences of opinion about details. In comparative mythology there was, with rare exceptions, no agreement at all about results beyond this point; Greek and Sanskrit, German and Slavonic myths were, in the immense majority of instances, to be regarded as mirror-pictures on earth, of celestial and meteorological phenomena. Thus even the story of the Earth Goddess, the Harvest Goddess, Demeter, was usually explained as a reflection in myth of one or another celestial phenomenon—dawn, storm-cloud, or something else according to taste.

Again, Greek or German myths were usually to be interpreted by comparison with myths in the Rig Veda. Their origin was to be

1

ascertained by discovering the Aryan root and original significance of the names of gods and heroes, such as Saranyu—Erinnys, Daphne—Dahanâ, Athene—Ahanâ. The etymology and meaning of such names being ascertained, the origin and sense of the myths in which the names occur should be clear.

Clear it was not. There were, in most cases, as many opinions as to the etymology and meaning of each name and myth, as there were philologists engaged in the study. Mannhardt, who began, in 1858, as a member of the philological school, in his last public utterance (1877) described the method and results, including his own work of 1858, as 'mainly failures.'

But, long ere that, the English cultivated public had, most naturally, accepted Mr. Max Müller as the representative of the school which then held the field in comparative mythology. His German and other foreign brethren, with their discrepant results, were only known to the general, in England (I am not speaking of English scholars), by the references to them in the Oxford professor's own works. His theories were made part of the education of children, and found their way into a kind of popular primers.

For these reasons, anyone in England who was daring enough to doubt, or to deny, the validity of the philological system of mythology in general was obliged to choose Mr. Max Müller as his adversary. He must strike, as it were, the shield of no Hospitaler of unsteady seat, but that of the Templar himself. And this is the cause of what seems to puzzle Mr. Max Müller, namely the attacks on his system and his results in particular. An English critic, writing for English readers, had to do with the scholar who chiefly represented the philological school of mythology in the eyes of England.

Autobiographical

Like other inquiring undergraduates in the sixties, I read such works on mythology as Mr. Max Müller had then given to the world; I read them with interest, but without conviction. The argument, the logic, seemed to evade one; it was purely, with me, a question of logic, for I was of course prepared to accept all of Mr. Max Müller's dicta on questions of etymologies. Even now I never venture to impugn them, only, as I observe that other scholars very frequently differ, toto cælo, from him and from each other in essential questions, I preserve a just balance of doubt; I wait till these gentlemen shall be at one among themselves.

After taking my degree in 1868, I had leisure to read a good

2

deal of mythology in the legends of all races, and found my distrust of Mr. Max Müller's reasoning increase upon me. The main cause was that whereas Mr. Max Müller explained Greek myths by etymologies of words in the Aryan languages, chiefly Greek, Latin, Slavonic, and Sanskrit, I kept finding myths very closely resembling those of Greece among Red Indians, Kaffirs, Eskimo, Samoyeds, Kamilaroi, Maoris, and Cahrocs. Now if Aryan myths arose from a 'disease' of Aryan languages, it certainly did seem an odd thing that myths so similar to these abounded where non-Aryan languages alone prevailed. Did a kind of linguistic measles affect all tongues alike, from Sanskrit to Choctaw, and everywhere produce the same ugly scars in religion and myth?

The Ugly Scars

The ugly scars were the problem! A civilised fancy is not puzzled for a moment by a beautiful beneficent Sun-god, or even by his beholding the daughters of men that they are fair. But a civilised fancy is puzzled when the beautiful Sun-god makes love in the shape of a dog.[8] To me, and indeed to Mr. Max Müller, the ugly scars were the problem.

He has written—'What makes mythology mythological, in the true sense of the word, is what is utterly unintelligible, absurd, strange, or miraculous.' But he explained these blots on the mythology of Greece, for example, as the result practically of old words and popular sayings surviving in languages after the original, harmless, symbolical meanings of the words and sayings were lost. What had been a poetical remark about an aspect of nature became an obscene, or brutal, or vulgar myth, a stumbling block to Greek piety and to Greek philosophy.

To myself, on the other hand, it seemed that the ugly scars were remains of that kind of taste, fancy, customary law, and incoherent speculation which everywhere, as far as we know, prevails to various degrees in savagery and barbarism. Attached to the 'hideous idols,' as Mr. Max Müller calls them, of early Greece, and implicated in a ritual which religious conservatism dared not abandon, the fables of perhaps neolithic ancestors of the Hellenes remained in the religion and the legends known to Plato and Socrates. That this process of 'survival' is a vera causa, illustrated in every phase of evolution, perhaps nobody denies.

Thus the phenomena which the philological school of

---

[8] Suidas, s.v. τελμισσεις; he cites Dionysius of Chalcis, B.C. 200.

mythology explains by a disease of language we would explain by survival from a savage state of society and from the mental peculiarities observed among savages in all ages and countries. Of course there is nothing new in this: I was delighted to discover the idea in Eusebius as in Fontenelle; while, for general application to singular institutions, it was a commonplace of the last century.[9] Moreover, the idea had been widely used by Dr. E. B. Tylor in Primitive Culture, and by Mr. McLennan in his Primitive Marriage and essays on Totemism.

My Criticism of Mr. Max Müller

This idea I set about applying to the repulsive myths of civilised races, and to Märchen, or popular tales, at the same time combating the theories which held the field—the theories of the philological mythologists as applied to the same matter. In journalism I criticised Mr. Max Müller, and I admit that, when comparing the mutually destructive competition of varying etymologies, I did not abstain from the weapons of irony and badinage. The opportunity was too tempting! But, in the most sober seriousness, I examined Mr. Max Müller's general statement of his system, his hypothesis of certain successive stages of language, leading up to the mythopœic confusion of thought. It was not a question of denying Mr. Max Müller's etymologies, but of asking whether he established his historical theory by evidence, and whether his inferences from it were logically deduced. The results of my examination will be found in the article 'Mythology' in the Encyclopædia Britannica, and in La Mythologie.[10] It did not appear to me that Mr. Max Müller's general theory was valid, logical, historically demonstrated, or self-consistent. My other writings on the topic are chiefly Custom and Myth, Myth, Ritual, and Religion (with French and Dutch translations, both much improved and corrected by the translators), and an introduction to Mrs. Hunt's translation of Grimm's Märchen.

Success of Anthropological Method

During fifteen years the ideas which I advocated seem to have had some measure of success. This is, doubtless, due not to myself, but to the works of Mr. J. G. Frazer and of Professor Robertson Smith. Both of these scholars descend intellectually from a man less

9 See Goguet, and Millar of Glasgow, and Voltaire.
10 Translated by M. Parmentier.

scholarly than they, but, perhaps, more original and acute than any of us, my friend the late Mr. J. F. McLennan. To Mannhardt also much is owed, and, of course, above all, to Dr. Tylor. These writers, like Mr. Farnell and Mr. Jevons recently, seek for the answer to mythological problems rather in the habits and ideas of the folk and of savages and barbarians than in etymologies and 'a disease of language.' There are differences of opinion in detail: I myself may think that 'vegetation spirits,' the 'corn spirit,' and the rest occupy too much space in the systems of Mannhardt, and other moderns. Mr. Frazer, again, thinks less of the evidence for Totems among 'Aryans' than I was inclined to do.[11] But it is not, perhaps, an overstatement to say that explanation of myths by analysis of names, and the lately overpowering predominance of the Dawn, and the Sun, and the Night in mythological hypothesis, have received a slight check. They do not hold the field with the superiority which was theirs in England between 1860 and 1880. This fact—a scarcely deniable fact—does not, of course, prove that the philological method is wrong, or that the Dawn is not as great a factor in myth as Mr. Max Müller believes himself to have proved it to be. Science is inevitably subject to shiftings of opinion, action, and reaction.

Mr. Max Müller's Reply

In this state of things Mr. Max Müller produces his Contributions to the Science of Mythology,[12] which I propose to criticise as far as it is, or may seem to me to be, directed against myself, or against others who hold practically much the same views as mine. I say that I attempt to criticise the book 'as far as it is, or may seem to me to be, directed against' us, because it is Mr. Max Müller's occasional habit to argue (apparently) around rather than with his opponents. He says 'we are told this or that'—something which he does not accept—but he often does not inform us as to who tells us, or where. Thus a reader does not know whom Mr. Max Müller is opposing, or where he can find the adversary's own statement in his own words. Yet it is usual in such cases, and it is, I think, expedient, to give chapter and verse. Occasionally I find that Mr. Max Müller is honouring me by alluding to observations of my own, but often no reference is given to an opponent's name or books, and we discover the passages in question by accident or research. This method will be found to cause certain inconveniences.

---

[11] See 'Totemism,' infra.
[12] Longmans.

THE STORY OF DAPHNE

Mr. Max Müller's Method in Controversy

As an illustration of the author's controversial methods, take his observations on my alleged attempt to account for the metamorphosis of Daphne into a laurel tree. When I read these remarks (i. p. 4) I said, 'Mr. Max Müller vanquishes me there,' for he gave no reference to my statement. I had forgotten all about the matter, I was not easily able to find the passage to which he alluded, and I supposed that I had said just what Mr. Max Müller seemed to me to make me say—no more, and no less. Thus:

'Mr. Lang, as usual, has recourse to savages, most useful when they are really wanted. He quotes an illustration from the South Pacific that Tuna, the chief of the eels, fell in love with Ina and asked her to cut off his head. When his head had been cut off and buried, two cocoanut trees sprang up from the brain of Tuna. How is this, may I ask, to account for the story of Daphne? Everybody knows that "stories of the growing of plants out of the scattered members of heroes may be found from ancient Egypt to the wigwams of the Algonquins," but these stories seem hardly applicable to Daphne, whose members, as far as I know, were never either severed or scattered.'

I thought, perhaps hastily, that I must have made the story of Tuna 'account for the story of Daphne.' Mr. Max Müller does not actually say that I did so, but I understood him in that sense, and recognised my error. But, some guardian genius warning me, I actually hunted up my own observations.[13] Well, I had never said (as I conceived my critic to imply) that the story of Tuna 'accounts for the story of Daphne.' That was what I had not said. I had observed, 'As to interchange of shape between men and women and plants, our information, so far as the lower races are concerned, is less copious'—than in the case of stones. I then spoke of plant totems of one kin with human beings, of plant-souls,[14] of Indian and Egyptian plants animated by human souls, of a tree which became a young man and made love to a Yurucari girl, of metamorphosis into vegetables in Samoa,[15] of an Ottawa myth in which a man became a

---

[13] M. R. R. i. 155-160.
[14] Tylor's Prim. Cult. i. 145.
[15] Turner's Samoa, p. 219.

6

plant of maize, and then of the story of Tuna.[16] Next I mentioned plants said to have sprung from dismembered gods and heroes. All this, I said, all of it, proves that savages mythically regard human life as on a level with vegetable no less than with animal life. 'Turning to the mythology of Greece, we see that the same rule holds good. Metamorphosis into plants and flowers is extremely common,' and I, of course, attributed the original idea of such metamorphoses to 'the general savage habit of "levelling up,"' of regarding all things in nature as all capable of interchanging their identities. I gave, as classical examples, Daphne, Myrrha, Hyacinth, Narcissus, and the sisters of Phaethon. Next I criticised Mr. Max Müller's theory of Daphne. But I never hinted that the isolated Mangaian story of Tuna, or the stories of plants sprung from mangled men, 'accounted,' by themselves, 'for the story of Daphne.'

Mr. Max Müller is not content with giving a very elaborate and interesting account of how the story of Tuna arose (i. 5-7). He keeps Tuna in hand, and, at the peroration of his vast work (ii. 831), warns us that, before we compare myths in unrelated languages, we need 'a very accurate knowledge of their dialects . . . to prevent accidents like that of Tuna mentioned in the beginning.' What accident? That I explained the myth of Daphne by the myth of Tuna? But that is precisely what I did not do. I explained the Greek myth of Daphne (1) as a survival from the savage mental habit of regarding men as on a level with stones, beasts, and plants; or (2) as a tale 'moulded by poets on the same model.'[17] The latter is the more probable case, for we find Daphne late, in artificial or mythographic literature, in Ovid and Hyginus. In Ovid the river god, Pentheus, changes Daphne into a laurel. In Hyginus she is not changed at all; the earth swallows her, and a laurel fills her place.

Now I really did believe—perhaps any rapid reader would have believed—when I read Mr. Max Müller, that I must have tried to account for the story of Daphne by the story of Tuna. I actually wrote in the first draft of this work that I had been in the wrong. Then I verified the reference which my critic did not give, with the result which the reader has perused. Never could a reader have found out what I did really say from my critic, for he does not usually when he deals with me give chapter and verse. This may avoid an air of personal bickering, but how inconvenient it is!

Let me not be supposed to accuse Mr. Max Müller of consciously misrepresenting me. Of that I need not say that he is absolutely incapable.   My argument merely took, in his

---

[16] Gill's Myths and Songs, p. 79.
[17] M. R. R. ii. 160.

consciousness, the form which is suggested in the passage cited from him.

Tuna and Daphne

To do justice to Mr. Max Müller, I will here state fully his view of the story of Tuna, and then go on to the story of Daphne. For the sake of accuracy, I take the liberty of borrowing the whole of his statement (i. 4-7):—

'I must dwell a little longer on this passage in order to show the real difference between the ethnological and the philological schools of comparative mythology.

'First of all, what has to be explained is not the growing up of a tree from one or the other member of a god or hero, but the total change of a human being or a heroine into a tree, and this under a certain provocation. These two classes of plant-legends must be carefully kept apart. Secondly, what does it help us to know that people in Mangaia believed in the change of human beings into trees, if we do not know the reason why? This is what we want to know; and without it the mere juxtaposition of stories apparently similar is no more than the old trick of explaining ignotum per ignotius. It leads us to imagine that we have learnt something, when we really are as ignorant as before.

'If Mr. A. Lang had studied the Mangaian dialect, or consulted scholars like the Rev. W. W. Gill—it is from his "Myths and Songs from the South Pacific" that he quotes the story of Tuna—he would have seen that there is no similarity whatever between the stories of Daphne and of Tuna. The Tuna story belongs to a very well known class of ætiological plant-stories, which are meant to explain a no longer intelligible name of a plant, such as Snakeshead, Stiefmütterchen, &c.; it is in fact a clear case of what I call disease of language, cured by the ordinary nostrum of folk-etymology. I have often been in communication with the Rev. W. W. Gill about these South Pacific myths and their true meaning. The preface to his collection of Myths and Songs from the South Pacific was written by me in 1876; and if Mr. A. Lang had only read the whole chapter which treats of these Tree-Myths (p. 77 seq.), he would easily have perceived the real character of the Tuna story, and would not have placed it in the same class as the Daphne story; he would have found that the white kernel of the cocoanut was, in Mangaia, called the "brains of Tuna," a name like many more such names which after a time require an explanation.

'Considering that "cocoanut" was used in Mangaia in the sense of head (testa), the kernel or flesh of it might well be called

8

the brain. If then the white kernel had been called Tuna's brain, we have only to remember that in Mangaia there are two kinds of cocoanut trees, and we shall then have no difficulty in understanding why these twin cocoanut trees were said to have sprung from the two halves of Tuna's brain, one being red in stem, branches, and fruit, whilst the other was of a deep green. In proof of these trees being derived from the head of Tuna, we are told that we have only to break the nut in order to see in the sprouting germ the two eyes and the mouth of Tuna, the great eel, the lover of Ina. For a full understanding of this very complicated myth more information has been supplied by Mr. Gill. Ina means moon; Ina-mae-aitu, the heroine of our story, means Ina-who-had-a-divine (aitu) lover, and she was the daughter of Kui, the blind. Tuna means eel, and in Mangaia it was unlawful for women to eat eels, so that even now, as Mr. Gill informs me, his converts turn away from this fish with the utmost disgust. From other stories about the origin of cocoanut trees, told in the same island, it would appear that the sprouts of the cocoanut were actually called eels' heads, while the skulls of warriors were called cocoanuts.

'Taking all these facts together, it is not difficult to imagine how the story of Tuna's brain grew up; and I am afraid we shall have to confess that the legend of Tuna throws but little light on the legend of Daphne or on the etymology of her name. No one would have a word to say against the general principle that much that is irrational, absurd, or barbarous in the Veda is a survival of a more primitive mythology anterior to the Veda. How could it be otherwise?'

Criticism of Tuna and Daphne

Now (1), as to Daphne, we are not invariably told that hers was a case of 'the total change of a heroine into a tree.' In Ovid[18] she is thus changed. In Hyginus, on the other hand, the earth swallows her, and a tree takes her place. All the authorities are late. Here I cannot but reflect on the scholarly method of Mannhardt, who would have examined and criticised all the sources for the tale before trying to explain it. However, Daphne was not mangled; a tree did not spring from her severed head or scattered limbs. She was metamorphosed, or was buried in earth, a tree springing up from the place.

(2) I think we do know why the people of Mangaia 'believe in the change of human beings into trees.' It is one among many

---

[18] Metam. i. 567.

examples of the savage sense of the intercommunity of all nature. 'Antiquity made its division between man and the world in a very different sort than do the moderns.'[19]   I illustrate this mental condition fully in M. R. R. i. 46-56.   Why savages adopt the major premise, 'Human life is on a level with the life of all nature,' philosophers explain in various ways.   Hume regards it as an extension to the universe of early man's own consciousness of life and personality.   Dr. Tylor thinks that the opinion rests upon 'a broad philosophy of nature.'[20]   M. Lefébure appeals to psychical phenomena as I show later (see 'Fetishism').   At all events, the existence of these savage metaphysics is a demonstrated fact.   I established it[21] before invoking it as an explanation of savage belief in metamorphosis.

(3) 'The Tuna story belongs to a very well known class of ætiological plant-stories' (ætiological: assigning a cause for the plant, its peculiarities, its name, &c.), 'which are meant to explain a no longer intelligible name of a plant, &c.'   I also say, 'these myths are nature-myths, so far as they attempt to account for a fact in nature—namely, for the existence of certain plants, and for their place in ritual.'[22]

The reader has before him Mr. Max Müller's view.   The white kernel of the cocoanut was locally styled 'the brains of Tuna.'   That name required explanation.   Hence the story about the fate of Tuna. Cocoanut was used in Mangaia in the sense of 'head' (testa).   So it is now in England.

See Bell's Life, passim, as 'The Chicken got home on the cocoanut.'

The Explanation

On the whole, either cocoanut kernels were called 'brains of Tuna' because 'cocoanut'='head,' and a head has brains—and, well, somehow I fail to see why brains of Tuna in particular!   Or, there being a story to the effect that the first cocoanut grew out of the head of the metamorphosed Tuna, the kernel was called his brains. But why was the story told, and why of Tuna?   Tuna was an eel, and women may not eat eels; and Ina was the moon, who, a Mangaian Selene, loved no Latmian shepherd, but an eel.   Seriously, I fail to understand Mr. Max Müller's explanation.   Given the problem, to

---

[19] Grimm, cited by Liebrecht in Zur Volkskunde, p. 17.
[20] Primitive Culture, i. 285.
[21] Op. cit. i. 46-81.
[22] M. R. R. i. 160.

explain a no longer intelligible plant-name—brains of Tuna—(applied not to a plant but to the kernel of a nut), this name is explained by saying that the moon, Ina, loved an eel, cut off his head at his desire, and buried it. Thence sprang cocoanut trees, with a fanciful likeness to a human face—face of Tuna—on the nut. But still, why Tuna? How could the moon love an eel, except on my own general principle of savage 'levelling up' of all life in all nature? In my opinion, the Mangaians wanted a fable to account for the resemblance of a cocoanut to the human head—a resemblance noted, as I show, in our own popular slang. The Mangaians also knew the moon, in her mythical aspect, as Ina; and Tuna, whatever his name may mean (Mr. Max Müller does not tell us), was an eel.[23] Having the necessary savage major premise in their minds, 'All life is on a level and interchangeable,' the Mangaians thought well to say that the head-like cocoanut sprang from the head of her lover, an eel, cut off by Ina. The myth accounts, I think, for the peculiarities of the cocoanut, rather than for the name 'brains of Tuna;' for we still ask, 'Why of Tuna in particular? Why Tuna more than Rangoa, or anyone else?'

'We shall have to confess that the legend of Tuna throws but little light on the legend of Daphne, or on the etymology of her name.'

I never hinted that the legend of Tuna threw light on the etymology of the name of Daphne. Mangaian and Greek are not allied languages. Nor did I give the Tuna story as an explanation of the Daphne story. I gave it as one in a mass of illustrations of the savage mental propensity so copiously established by Dr. Tylor in Primitive Culture. The two alternative explanations which I gave of the Daphne story I have cited. No mention of Tuna occurs in either.

Disease of Language and Folk-etymology

The Tuna story is described as 'a clear case of disease of language cured by the ordinary nostrum of folk-etymology.' The 'disease' showed itself, I suppose, in the presence of the Mangaian words for 'brain of Tuna.' But the story of Tuna gives no folk-etymology of the name Tuna. Now, to give an etymology of a name of forgotten meaning is the sole object of folk-etymology. The plant-name, 'snake's head,' given as an example by Mr. Max Müller,

---

[23] Erratum: This is erroneous. See Contributions, &c., vol. i. p. 6, where Mr. Max Müller writes, 'Tuna means eel.' This shows why Tuna, i.e. Eel, is the hero. His connection, as an admirer, with the Moon, perhaps remains obscure.

needs no etymological explanation. A story may be told to explain why the plant is called snake's head, but a story to give an etymology of snake's head is superfluous. The Tuna story explains why the cocoanut kernel is called 'brains of Tuna,' but it offers no etymology of Tuna's name. On the other hand, the story that marmalade (really marmalet) is so called because Queen Mary found comfort in marmalade when she was sea-sick—hence Marie-malade, hence marmalade—gives an etymological explanation of the origin of the word marmalade. Here is a real folk-etymology. We must never confuse such myths of folk-etymology with myths arising (on the philological hypothesis) from 'disease of language.' Thus, Daphne is a girl pursued by Apollo, and changed into a daphne plant or laurel, or a laurel springs from the earth where she was buried. On Mr. Max Müller's philological theory Daphne=Dahanâ, and meant 'the burning one.' Apollo may be derived from a Sanskrit form, *Apa-var-yan, or *Apa-val-yan (though how Greeks ever heard a Sanskrit word, if such a word as Apa-val-yan ever existed, we are not told), and may mean 'one who opens the gate of the sky' (ii. 692-696).[24] At some unknown date the ancestors of the Greeks would say 'The opener of the gates of the sky (*Apa-val-yan, i.e. the sun) pursues the burning one (Dahanâ, i.e. the dawn).' The Greek language would retain this poetic saying in daily use till, in the changes of speech, *Apa-val-yan ceased to be understood, and became Apollo, while Dahanâ ceased to be understood, and became Daphne. But the verb being still understood, the phrase ran, 'Apollo pursues Daphne.' Now the Greeks had a plant, laurel, called daphne. They therefore blended plant, daphne, and heroine's name, Daphne, and decided that the phrase 'Apollo pursues Daphne' meant that Apollo chased a nymph, Daphne, who, to escape his love, turned into a laurel. I cannot give Mr. Max Müller's theory of the Daphne story more clearly. If I misunderstand it, that does not come from want of pains.

In opposition to it we urge that (1) the etymological equations, Daphne=Dahanâ, Apollo=*Apa-val-yan, are not generally accepted by other scholars. Schröder, in fact, derives Apollo 'from the Vedic Saparagenya, "worshipful," an epithet of Agni,' who is Fire (ii. 688), and so on. Daphne=Dahanâ is no less doubted. Of course a Greek simply cannot be 'derived' from a Sanskrit word, as is stated, though both may have a common origin, just as French is not 'derived from' Italian.

---

[24] Phonetically there may be 'no possible objection to the derivation of Απολλων from a Sanskrit form, *Apa-var-yan, or *Apa-val-yan' (ii. 692); but, historically, Greek is not derived from Sanskrit surely!

(2) If the etymologies were accepted, no proof is offered to us of the actual existence, as a vera causa, of the process by which a saying. 'Apollo pursues Daphne,' remains in language, while the meaning of the words is forgotten. This process is essential, but undemonstrated. See the chapter here on 'The Riddle Theory.'

(3) These processes, if demonstrated, which they are not, must be carefully discriminated from the actual demonstrable process of folk-etymology. The Marmalade legend gives the etymology of a word, marmalade; the Daphne legend does not give an etymology.

(4) The theory of Daphne is of the kind protested against by Mannhardt, where he warns us against looking in most myths for a 'mirror-picture' on earth of celestial phenomena.[25] For these reasons, among others, I am disinclined to accept Mr. Max Müller's attempt to explain the story of Daphne.

Mannhardt on Daphne

Since we shall presently find Mr. Max Müller claiming the celebrated Mannhardt as a sometime deserter of philological comparative mythology, who 'returned to his old colours,' I observe with pleasure that Mannhardt is on my side and against the Oxford Professor. Mannhardt shows that the laurel (daphne) was regarded as a plant which, like our rowan tree, averts evil influences. 'Moreover, the laurel, like the Maibaum, was looked on as a being with a spirit. This is the safest result which myth analysis can extract from the story of Daphne, a nymph pursued by Apollo and changed into a laurel. It is a result of the use of the laurel in his ritual.'[26] In 1877, a year after Mannhardt is said by Mr. Max Müller to have returned to his old colours, he repeats this explanation.[27] In the same work (p. 20) he says that 'there is no reason for accepting Max Müller's explanation about the Sun-god and the Dawn, wo jeder thätliche Anhalt dafür fehlt.' For this opinion we might also cite the Sanskrit scholars Whitney and Bergaigne.[28]

---

[25] Mythologische Forschungen, p. 275.
[26] Baumkultus, p. 297. Berlin: 1875.
[27] Antike Wald- und Feldkulte, p. 257. Referring to Baumkultus, p. 297.
[28] Oriental and Linguistic Studies, second series, p. 160. La Religion Védique, iii. 293.

THE QUESTION OF ALLIES

Athanasius

Mr. Max Müller protests, most justly, against the statement that he, like St. Athanasius, stands alone, contra mundum. If ever this phrase fell from my pen (in what connection I know not), it is as erroneous as the position of St. Athanasius is honourable. Mr. Max Müller's ideas, in various modifications, are doubtless still the most prevalent of any. The anthropological method has hardly touched, I think, the learned contributors to Roscher's excellent mythological Lexicon. Dr. Brinton, whose American researches are so useful, seems decidedly to be a member of the older school. While I do not exactly remember alluding to Athanasius, I fully and freely withdraw the phrase. But there remain questions of allies to be discussed.

Italian Critics

Mr. Max Müller asks,[29] 'What would Mr. Andrew Lang say if he read the words of Signer Canizzaro, in his "Genesi ed Evoluzione del Mito" (1893), "Lang has laid down his arms before his adversaries"?' Mr. Lang 'would smile.' And what would Mr. Max Müller say if he read the words of Professor Enrico Morselli, 'Lang gives no quarter to his adversaries, who, for the rest, have long been reduced to silence'?[30] The Right Hon. Professor also smiles, no doubt. We both smile. Solvuntur risu tabulæ.

A Dutch Defender

The question of the precise attitude of Professor Tiele, the accomplished Gifford Lecturer in the University of Edinburgh (1897), is more important and more difficult. His remarks were made in 1885, in an essay on the Myth of Cronos, and were separately reprinted, in 1886, from the 'Revue de l'Histoire des Religions,' which I shall cite. Where they refer to myself they deal with Custom and Myth, not with Myth, Ritual, and Religion (1887). It seems best to quote, ipsissimis verbis, Mr. Max Müller's comments on Professor Tiele's remarks. He writes (i. viii.):

---

[29] 1, viii. cf. i. 27.
[30] Riv. Crit. Mensile. Geneva, iii. xiv. p. 2.

'Let us proceed next to Holland. Professor Tiele, who had actually been claimed as an ally of the victorious army, declares:— "Je dois m'élever, au nom de la science mythologique et de l'exactitude . . . centre une méthode qui ne fait que glisser sur des problèmes de première importance." (See further on, p. 35.)

'And again:

'"Ces braves gens qui, pour peu qu'ils aient lu un ou deux livres de mythologie et d'anthropologie, et un ou deux récits de voyages, ne manqueront pas de se mettre à comparer à tort et à travers, et pour tout résultat produiront la confusion.""

Again (i. 35):

'Besides Signer Canizzaro and Mr. Horatio Hale, the veteran among comparative ethnologists, Professor Tiele, in his Le Mythe de Kronos (1886), has very strongly protested against the downright misrepresentations of what I and my friends have really written.

'Professor Tiele had been appealed to as an unimpeachable authority. He was even claimed as an ally by the ethnological students of customs and myths, but he strongly declined that honour (1. c., p. 31):-

'"M. Lang m'a fait 1'honneur de me citer," he writes, "comme un de ses alliés, et j'ai lieu de croire que M. Gaidoz en fait en quelque mesure autant. Ces messieurs n'ont point entièrement tort. Cependant je dois m'élever, au nom de la science mythologique et de 1'exactitude dont elle ne peut pas plus se passer que les autres sciences, contre une méthode qui ne fait que glisser sur des problèmes de première importance," &c.

'Speaking of the whole method followed by those who actually claimed to have founded a new school of mythology, he says (p. 21):—

'"Je crains toutefois que ce qui s'y trouve de vrai ne soit connu depuis longtemps, et que la nouvelle école ne pèche par exclusionisme tout autant que les aînées qu'elle combat avec tant de conviction."

'That is exactly what I have always said. What is there new in comparing the customs and myths of the Greeks with those of the barbarians? Has not even Plato done this? Did anybody doubt that the Greeks, nay even the Hindus, were uncivilised or savages, before they became civilised or tamed? Was not this common-sense view, so strongly insisted on by Fontenelle and Vico in the eighteenth century, carried even to excess by such men as De Brosses (1709-1771)? And have the lessons taught to De Brosses by his witty contemporaries been quite forgotten? Must his followers be told again and again that they ought to begin with a critical examination of the evidence put before them by casual travellers, and that

15

mythology is as little made up of one and the same material as the crust of the earth of granite only?'

Reply

Professor Tiele wrote in 1885. I do not remember having claimed his alliance, though I made one or two very brief citations from his remarks on the dangers of etymology applied to old proper names.[31] To citations made by me later in 1887 Professor Tiele cannot be referring.[32] Thus I find no proof of any claim of alliance put forward by me, but I do claim a right to quote the Professor's published words. These I now translate:—[33]

'What goes before shows adequately that I am an ally, much more than an adversary, of the new school, whether styled ethnological or anthropological. It is true that all the ideas advanced by its partisans are not so new as they seem. Some of us— I mean among those who, without being vassals of the old school, were formed by it—had not only remarked already the defects of the reigning method, but had perceived the direction in which researches should be made; they had even begun to say so. This does not prevent the young school from enjoying the great merit of having first formulated with precision, and with the energy of conviction, that which had hitherto been but imperfectly pointed out. If henceforth mythological science marches with a firmer foot, and loses much of its hypothetical character, it will in part owe this to the stimulus of the new school.'

'Braves Gens'

Professor Tiele then bids us leave our cries of triumph to the servum imitatorum pecus, braves gens, and so forth, as in the passage which Mr. Max Müller, unless I misunderstand him, regards as referring to the 'new school,' and, notably, to M. Gaidoz and myself, though such language ought not to apply to M. Gaidoz, because he is a scholar. I am left to uncovenanted mercies.

Professor Tiele on Our Merits

The merits of the new school Professor Tiele had already stated:—[34]

---

[31] Custom and Myth, p. 3, citing Revue de l'Hist. des Religions, ii. 136.
[32] M. R. R. i. 24.
[33] Revue de l'Hist. des Religions, xii. 256.
[34] Op. cit. p. 253.

'If I were reduced to choose between this method and that of comparative philology, I would prefer the former without the slightest hesitation. This method alone enables us to explain the fact, such a frequent cause of surprise, that the Greeks like the Germans . . . could attribute to their gods all manner of cruel, cowardly and dissolute actions. This method alone reveals the cause of all the strange metamorphoses of gods into animals, plants, and even stones. . . . In fact, this method teaches us to recognise in all these oddities the survivals of an age of barbarism long overpast, but lingering into later times, under the form of religious legends, the most persistent of all traditions. . . . This method, enfin, can alone help us to account for the genesis of myths, because it devotes itself to studying them in their rudest and most primitive shape. . . .'

Destruction and Construction

Thus writes Professor Tiele about the constructive part of our work. As to the destructive—or would-be destructive—part, he condenses my arguments against the method of comparative philology. 'To resume, the whole house of comparative philological mythology is builded on the sand, and her method does not deserve confidence, since it ends in such divergent results.' That is Professor Tiele's statement of my destructive conclusions, and he adds, 'So far, I have not a single objection to make. I can still range myself on Mr. Lang's side when he' takes certain distinctions into which it is needless to go here.[35]

Allies or Not?

These are several of the passages on which, in 1887, I relied as evidence of the Professor's approval, which, I should have added, is only partial It is he who, unsolicited, professes himself 'much more our ally than our adversary.' It is he who proclaims that Mr. Max Midler's central hypothesis is erroneous, and who makes 'no objection' to my idea that it is 'builded on the sand.' It is he who assigns essential merits to our method, and I fail to find that he 'strongly declines the honour' of our alliance. The passage about 'braves gens' explicitly does not refer to us.

---

[35] Op. cit. xii. 250.

17

Our Errors

In 1887, I was not careful to quote what Professor Tiele had said against us. First, as to our want of novelty. That merit, I think, I had never claimed. I was proud to point out that we had been anticipated by Eusebius of Cæsarea, by Fontenelle, and doubtless by many others. We repose, as Professor Tiele justly says, on the researches of Dr. Tylor. At the same time it is Professor Tiele who constantly speaks of 'the new school,' while adding that he himself had freely opposed Mr. Max Müller's central hypothesis, 'a disease of language,' in Dutch periodicals. The Professor also censures our 'exclusiveness,' our 'narrowness,' our 'songs of triumph,' our use of parody (M. Gaidoz republished an old one, not to my own taste; I have also been guilty of 'The Great Gladstone Myth') and our charge that our adversaries neglect ethnological material. On this I explain myself later.[36]

Uses of Philology

Our method (says Professor Tiele) 'cannot answer all the questions which the science of mythology must solve, or, at least, must study.' Certainly it makes no such pretence.

Professor Tiele then criticises Sir George Cox and Mr. Robert Brown, junior, for their etymologies of Poseidon. Indiscreet followers are not confined to our army alone. Now, the use of philology, we learn, is to discourage such etymological vagaries as those of Sir G. Cox.[37] We also discourage them—severely. But we are warned that philology really has discovered 'some undeniably certain etymologies' of divine names. Well, I also say, 'Philology alone can tell whether Zeus Asterios, or Adonis, or Zeus Labrandeus is originally a Semitic or a Greek divine name; here she is the Pythoness we must all consult.'[38] And is it my fault that, even in this matter, the Pythonesses utter such strangely discrepant oracles? Is Athene from a Zend root (Benfey), a Greek root (Curtius), or to be interpreted by Sanskrit Ahanâ (Max Müller)? Meanwhile Professor Tiele repeats that, in a search for the origin of myths, and, above all, of obscene and brutal myths, 'philology will lead us far from our aim.' Now, if the school of Mr. Max Müller has a mot d'ordre, it is, says Professor Tiele, 'to call mythology a disease of language.'[39] But,

---

[36] P. 104, infra.
[37] Revue de l'Hist. des Religions, xii. 259.
[38] M. R. R. i. 25.
[39] Rev. xii. 247.

adds Mr. Max Müller's learned Dutch defender, mythologists, while using philology for certain purposes, 'must shake themselves free, of course, from the false hypothesis' (Mr. Max Müller's) 'which makes of mythology a mere maladie du langage.' This professor is rather a dangerous defender of Mr. Max Müller! He removes the very corner-stone of his edifice, which Tiele does not object to our describing as founded on the sand. Mr. Max Müller does not cite (as far as I observe) these passages in which Professor Tiele (in my view, and in fact) abandons (for certain uses) his system of mythology. Perhaps Professor Tiele has altered his mind, and, while keeping what Mr. Max Müller quotes, braves gens, and so on, has withdrawn what he said about 'the false hypothesis of a disease of language.' But my own last book about myths was written in 1886-1887, shortly after Professor Tiele's remarks were published (1886) as I have cited them.

Personal Controversy

All this matter of alliances may seem, and indeed is, of a personal character, and therefore unimportant. Professor Tiele's position in 1885-86 is clearly defined. Whatever he may have published since, he then accepted the anthropological or ethnological method, as alone capable of doing the work in which we employ it. This method alone can discover the origin of ancient myths, and alone can account for the barbaric element, that old puzzle, in the myths of civilised races. This the philological method, useful for other purposes, cannot do, and its central hypothesis can only mislead us. I was not aware, I repeat, that I ever claimed Professor Tiele's 'alliance,' as he, followed by Mr. Max Müller, declares. They cannot point, as a proof of an assertion made by Professor Tiele, 1885-86, to words of mine which did not see the light till 1887, in Myth, Ritual, and Religion, i. pp. 24, 43, 44. Not that I deny Professor Tiele's statement about my claim of his alliance before 1885-86. I merely ask for a reference to this claim. In 1887[40] I cited his observations (already quoted) on the inadequate and misleading character of the philological method, when we are seeking for 'the origin of a myth, or the physical explanation of the oldest myths, or trying to account for the rude and obscene element in the divine legends of civilised races.' I added the Professor's applause of the philological method as applied to other problems of mythology; for example, 'the genealogical relations of myths. . . . The philological method alone can answer

---

[40] M. R. R. i. 24.

19

here,' aided, doubtless, by historical and archæological researches as to the inter-relations of races. This approval of the philological method, I cited; the reader will find the whole passage in the Revue, vol. xii. p. 260. I remarked, however, that this will seem 'a very limited province,' though, in this province, 'Philology is the Pythoness we must all consult; in this sphere she is supreme, when her high priests are of one mind.' Thus I did not omit to notice Professor Tiele's comments on the merits of the philological method. To be sure, he himself does not apply it when he comes to examine the Myth of Cronos. 'Are the God and his myth original or imported? I have not approached this question because it does not seem to me ripe in this particular case.'[41] 'Mr. Lang has justly rejected the opinion of Welcker and Mr. Max Müller, that Cronos is simply formed from Zeus's epithet, κρονιων.'[42] This opinion, however, Mr. Max Müller still thinks the 'most likely' (ii. 507).

My other citation of Professor Tiele in 1887 says that our pretensions 'are not unacknowledged' by him, and, after a long quotation of approving passages, I add 'the method is thus applauded by a most competent authority, and it has been warmly accepted' (pray note the distinction) by M. Gaidoz.[43] I trust that what I have said is not unfair. Professor Tiele's objections, not so much to our method as to our manners, and to my own use of the method in a special case, have been stated, or will be stated later. Probably I should have put them forward in 1887; I now repair my error. My sole wish is to be fair; if Mr. Max Müller has not wholly succeeded in giving the full drift of Professor Tiele's remarks, I am certain that it is from no lack of candour.

The Story of Cronos

Professor Tiele now devotes fifteen pages to the story of Cronos, and to my essay on that theme. He admits that I was right in regarding the myth as 'extraordinarily old,' and that in Greece it must go back to a period when Greeks had not passed the New Zealand level of civilisation. [Now, the New Zealanders were cannibals!] But 'we are the victims of a great illusion if we think that a mere comparison of a Maori and Greek myth explains the myth.' I only profess to explain the savagery of the myth by the fact (admitted) that it was composed by savages. The Maori story 'is a myth of the creation of light.' I, for my part, say, 'It is a myth of the

[41] Rev. xii. 277.
[42] Rev. xii. 264.
[43] M. R. R. i. 44, 45.

severance of heaven and earth.'[44] And so it is! No Being said, in Maori, 'Fiat lux!' Light is not here created. Heaven lay flat on Earth, all was dark, somebody kicked Heaven up, the already existing light came in. Here is no création de la lumière. I ask Professor Tiele, 'Do you, sir, create light when you open your window-shutters in the morning? No, you let light in!' The Maori tale is also 'un mythe primitif de l'aurore,' a primitive dawn myth. Dawn, again! Here I lose Professor Tiele.

'Has the myth of Cronos the same sense?' Probably not, as the Maori story, to my mind, has not got it either. But Professor Tiele says, 'The myth of Cronos has precisely the opposite sense.'[45] What is the myth of Cronos? Ouranos (Heaven) married Gaea (Earth). Ouranos 'hid his children from the light in the hollows of Earth' (Hesiod). So, too, the New Zealand gods were hidden from light while Heaven (Rangi) lay flat on Papa (Earth). The children 'were concealed between the hollows of their parent's breasts.' They did not like it, for they dwelt in darkness. So Cronos took an iron sickle and mutilated Ouranos in such a way, enfin, as to divorce him a thoro. 'Thus,' I say, 'were Heaven and Earth practically divorced.' The Greek gods now came out of the hollows where they had been, like the New Zealand gods, 'hidden from the light.'

Professor Tiele on Sunset Myths

No, says Professor Tiele, 'the story of Cronos has precisely the opposite meaning.' The New Zealand myth is one of dawn, the Greek myth is one of sunset. The mutilated part of poor Ouranos is le phallus du ciel, le soleil, which falls into 'the Cosmic ocean,' and then, of course, all is dark. Professor Tiele may be right here; I am indifferent. All that I wanted to explain was the savage complexion of the myth, and Professor Tiele says that I have explained that, and (xii. 264) he rejects the etymological theory of Mr. Max Müller.

I say that, in my opinion, the second part of the Cronos myth (the child-swallowing performances of Cronos) 'was probably a world-wide Märchen, or tale, attracted into the cycle of which Cronos was the centre, without any particular reason beyond the law which makes detached myths crystallise round any celebrated name.'

Professor Tiele says he does not grasp the meaning of, or believe in, any such law. Well, why is the world-wide tale of the Cyclops told about Odysseus? It is absolutely out of keeping, and it

---

[44] Custom and Myth, p. 51.
[45] Rev. xii. 262.

puzzles commentators. In fact, here was a hero and there was a tale, and the tale was attracted into the cycle of the hero; the very last man to have behaved as Odysseus is made to do.[46] But Cronos was an odious ruffian. The world-wide tale of swallowing and disgorging the children was attracted to his too notorious name 'by grace of congruity.' Does Professor Tiele now grasp my meaning (saisir)?

Our Lack of Scientific Exactness

I do not here give at full length Professor Tiele's explanation of the meaning of a myth which I do not profess to explain myself. Thus, drops of the blood of Ouranos falling on Earth begat the Mélies, usually rendered 'Nymphs of the Ash-trees.' But Professor Tiele says they were really bees (Hesychius, μελιαι=μελισσαι)—'that is to say, stars.' Everybody has observed that the stars rise up off the earth, like the bees sprung from the blood of Ouranos. In Myth, Ritual, and Religion (i. 299-315) I give the competing explanations of Mr. Max Müller, of Schwartz (Cronos=storm god), Preller (Cronos=harvest god), of others who see the sun, or time, in Cronos; while, with Professor Tiele, Cronos is the god of the upper air, and also of the underworld and harvest; he 'doubles the part.' 'Il est l'un et l'autre'—that is, 'le dieu qui fait mûrir le blé' and also 'un dieu des lieux souterrains.' 'Il habite les profondeurs sous la terre,' he is also le dieu du ciel nocturne.

It may have been remarked that I declined to add to this interesting collection of plausible explanations of Cronos. A selection of such explanations I offer in tabular form:—

Cronos was God of

Time (?)—Max Müller
Sun—Sayce
Midnight sky—Kuhn

Under-world }
Midnight sky}—Tiele
Harvest }

Harvest—Preller
Storm—Schwartz
Star-swallowing sky—Canon Taylor
Sun scorching spring—Hartung

---

[46] Odyssey, book ix.

Cronos was by Race

Late Greek (?)—Max Müller
Semitic—Böttiger
Accadian (?)—Sayce

Etymology of Cronos

Χρονος=Time (?)—Max Müller
Krāna (Sanskrit)—Kuhn
Karnos (Horned)—Brown
κραινω—Preller

The pleased reader will also observe that the phallus of Ouranos is the sun (Tiele), that Cronos is the sun (Sayce), that Cronos mutilating Ouranos is the sun (Hartung), just as the sun is the mutilated part of Ouranos (Tiele); Or is, according to others, the stone which Cronos swallowed, and which acted as an emetic.

My Lack of Explanation of Cronos

Now, I have offered no explanation at all of who Cronos was, what he was god of, from what race he was borrowed, from what language his name was derived. The fact is that I do not know the truth about these important debated questions. Therefore, after speaking so kindly of our method, and rejecting the method of Mr. Max Müller, Professor Tiele now writes thus (and this Mr. Max Müller does cite, as we have seen):—

'Mr. Lang and M. Gaidoz are not entirely wrong in claiming me as an ally. But I must protest, in the name of mythological science, and of the exactness as necessary to her as to any of the other sciences, against a method which only glides over questions of the first importance' (name, origin, province, race of Cronos), 'and which to most questions can only reply, with a smile, C'est chercher raison où il n'y en a pas.'

My Crime

Now, what important questions was I gliding over? In what questions did I not expect to find reason? Why in this savage fatras about Cronos swallowing his children, about blood-drops becoming bees (Mr. Max Müller says 'Melian nymphs'), and bees being stars, and all the rest of a prehistoric Märchen worked over again and again by the later fancy of Greek poets and by Greek voyagers who recognised Cronos in Moloch. In all this I certainly saw no 'reason,'

23

but I have given in tabular form the general, if inharmonious, conclusions of more exact and conscientious scholars, 'their variegated hypotheses,' as Mannhardt says in the case of Demeter. My error, rebuked by Professor Tiele, is the lack of that 'scientific exactitude' exhibited by the explanations arranged in my tabular form.

My Reply to Professor Tiele

I would reply that I am not engaged in a study of the Cult of Cronos, but of the revolting element in his Myth: his swallowing of his children, taking a stone emetic by mistake, and disgorging the swallowed children alive; the stone being on view at Delphi long after the Christian era. Now, such stories of divine feats of swallowing and disgorging are very common, I show, in savage myth and popular Märchen. The bushmen have Kwai Hemm, who swallows the sacred Mantis insect. He is killed, and all the creatures whom he has swallowed return to light. Such stories occur among Australians, Kaffirs, Red Men, in Guiana, in Greenland, and so on. In some cases, among savages. Night (conceived as a person), or one star which obscures another star, is said to 'swallow' it. Therefore, I say, 'natural phenomena, explained on savage principles, might give the data of the swallowing myth, of Cronos'[47]—that is, the myth of Cronos may be, probably is, originally a nature-myth. 'On this principle Cronos would be (ad hoc) the Night.' Professor Tiele does not allude to this effort at interpretation. But I come round to something like the view of Kuhn. Cronos (ad hoc) is the midnight [sky], which Professor Tiele also regards as one of his several aspects. It is not impossible, I think, that if the swallowing myth was originally a nature-myth, it was suggested by Night. But the question I tried to answer was, 'Why did the Greeks, of all people, tell such a disgusting story?' And I replied, with Professor Tiele's approval, that they inherited it from an age to which such follies were natural, an age when the ancestors of the Greeks were on (or under) the Maori stage of culture. Now, the Maoris, a noble race, with poems of great beauty and speculative power, were cannibals, like Cronos. To my mind, 'scientific exactitude' is rather shown in confessing ignorance than in adding to the list of guesses.

---

[47] C. and M. p. 56.

Conclusion as to Professor Tiele

The learned Professor's remarks on being 'much more my ally than my opponent' were published before my Myth, Ritual, and Religion, in which (i. 24, 25) I cited his agreement with me in the opinion that 'the philological method' (Mr. Max Müller's) is 'inadequate and misleading, when it is a question of discovering the origin of a myth.' I also quoted his unhesitating preference of ours to Mr. Max Müller's method (i. 43, 44). I did not cite a tithe of what he actually did say to our credit. But I omitted to quote what it was inexcusable not to add, that Professor Tiele thinks us 'too exclusive,' that he himself had already, before us, combated Mr. Max Müller's method in Dutch periodicals, that he blamed our 'songs of triumph' and our levities, that he thought we might have ignorant camp-followers, that I glided over important questions (bees, blood-drops, stars, Melian nymphs, the phallus of Ouranos, &c.), and showed scientific inexactitude in declining chercher raison où il n'y en a pas.

None the less, in Professor Tiele's opinion, our method is new (or is not new), illuminating, successful, and alone successful, for the ends to which we apply it, and, finally, we have shown Mr. Max Müller's method to be a house builded on the sand. That is the gist of what Professor Tiele said.

Mr. Max Müller, like myself, quotes part and omits part. He quotes twice Professor Tiele's observations on my deplorable habit of gliding over important questions. He twice says that we have 'actually' claimed the Professor as 'an ally of the victorious army,' 'the ethnological students of custom and myth,' and once adds, 'but he strongly declined that honour.' He twice quotes the famous braves gens passage, excepting only M. Gaidoz, as a scholar, from a censure explicitly directed at our possible camp-followers as distinguished from ourselves.

But if Mr. Max Müller quotes Professor Tiele's remarks proving that, in his opinion, the 'army' is really victorious; if he cites the acquiescence in my opinion that his mythological house is 'builded on the sands,' or Professor Tiele's preference for our method over his own, or Professor Tiele's volunteered remark that he is 'much more our ally than our adversary,' I have not detected the passages in Contributions to the Science of Mythology.

The reader may decide as to the relative importance of what I left out, and of what Mr. Max Müller omitted. He says, 'Professor Tiele and I differ on several points, but we perfectly understand each other, and when we have made a mistake we readily confess and correct it' (i. 37).

The two scholars, I thought, differed greatly. Mr. Max

Müller's war-cry, slogan, mot d'ordre, is to Professor Tiele 'a false hypothesis.' Our method, which Mr. Max Müller combats so bravely, is all that Professor Tiele has said of it. But, if all this is not conspicuously apparent in our adversary's book, it does not become me to throw the first stone. We are all, in fact, inclined unconsciously to overlook what makes against our argument. I have done it; and, to the best of my belief, Mr. Max Müller has not avoided the same error.

MANNHARDT

Mannhardt's Attitude

Professor Tiele, it may appear, really 'fights for his own hand,' and is not a thorough partisan of either side. The celebrated Mannhardt, too, doubtless the most original student of folk-lore since Grimm, might, at different periods of his career, have been reckoned an ally, now by philologists, now by 'the new school.' He may be said, in fact, to have combined what is best in the methods of both parties. Both are anxious to secure such support as his works can lend.

Moral Character Impeached

Mr. Max Müller avers that his moral character seems to be 'aimed at' by critics who say that he has no right to quote Mannhardt or Oldenberg as his supporters (1. xvi.). Now, without making absurd imputations, I do not reckon Mannhardt a thorough partisan of Mr. Max Müller. I could not put our theory so well as Mannhardt puts it. 'The study of the lower races is an invaluable instrument for the interpretation of the survivals from earlier stages, which we meet in the full civilisation of cultivated peoples, but which arose in the remotest fetishism and savagery.'

Like Mr. Max Müller, I do not care for the vague word 'fetishism,' otherwise Mannhardt's remark exactly represents my own position, the anthropological position.[48] Now, Mr. Max Müller does not like that position. That position he assails. It was Mannhardt's, however, when he wrote the book quoted, and, so far, Mannhardt was not absolutely one of Mr. Max Müller's 'supporters'—unless I am one. 'I have even been accused,' says Mr. Max Müller, 'of intentionally ignoring or suppressing Mannhardt's labours. How charitable!' (1. xvii.) I trust, from our author's use of the word todtschweigen, that this uncharitable charge was made in Germany.

Mannhardt

Mannhardt, for a time, says Mr. Max Müller, 'expressed his mistrust in some of the results of comparative mythology' (1. xvii.).

---

[48] W. u. F. K. xxiii.

Indeed, I myself quote him to that very effect.[49] Not only 'some of the results,' but the philological method itself was distrusted by Mannhardt, as by Curtius. 'The failure of the method in its practical working lies in a lack of the historical sense,' says Mannhardt.[50] Mr. Max Müller may have, probably has, referred to these sayings of Mannhardt; or, if he has not, no author is obliged to mention everybody who disagrees with him. Mannhardt's method was mainly that of folklore, not of philology. He examined peasant customs and rites as 'survivals' of the oldest paganism. Mr. Frazer applies Mannhardt's rich lore to the explanation of Greek and other rites in The Golden Bough, that entrancing book. Such was Mannhardt's position (as I shall prove at large) when he was writing his most famous works. But he 'returned at last to his old colours' (1. xvii.) in Die lettischen Sonnenmythen (1875). In 1880 Mannhardt died. Mr. Max Müller does not say whether Mannhardt, before a decease deeply regretted, recanted his heretical views about the philological method, and his expressed admiration of the study of the lower races as 'an invaluable instrument.' One would gladly read a recantation so important. But Mr. Max Müller does tell us that 'if I did not refer to his work in my previous contributions to the science of mythology the reason was simple enough. It was not, as has been suggested, my wish to suppress it (todtschweigen), but simply my want of knowledge of the materials with which he dealt' (German popular customs and traditions) 'and therefore the consciousness of my incompetence to sit in judgment on his labours.' Again, we are told that there was no need of criticism or praise of Mannhardt. He had Mr. Frazer as his prophet—but not till ten years after his death.

Mannhardt's Letters

'Mannhardt's state of mind with regard to the general principles of comparative philology has been so exactly my own,' says Mr. Max Müller, that he cites Mannhardt's letters to prove the fact. But as to the application to myth of the principles of comparative philology, Mannhardt speaks of 'the lack of the historical sense' displayed in the practical employment of the method. This, at least, is 'not exactly' Mr. Max Müller's own view. Probably he refers to the later period when Mannhardt 'returned to his old colours.'

---

[49] M. R. R. i. 23.
[50] W. u. F. K. xvii.

28

The letters of Mannhardt, cited in proof of his exact agreement with Mr. Max Müller about comparative philology, do not, as far as quoted, mention the subject of comparative philology at all (1. xviii-xx.). Possibly 'philology' is here a slip of the pen, and 'mythology' may be meant.

Mannhardt says to Müllenhoff (May 2, 1876) that he has been uneasy 'at the extent which sun myths threaten to assume in my comparisons.' He is opening 'a new point of view;' materials rush in, 'so that the sad danger seemed inevitable of everything becoming everything.' In Mr. Max Müller's own words, written long ago, he expressed his dread, not of 'everything becoming everything' (a truly Heraclitean state of affairs), but of the 'omnipresent Sun and the inevitable Dawn appearing in ever so many disguises.' 'Have we not,' he asks, 'arrived both at the same conclusion?' Really, I do not know! Had Mannhardt quite cashiered 'the corn-spirit,' who, perhaps, had previously threatened to 'become everything'? He is still in great vigour, in Mr. Frazer's Golden Bough, and Mr. Frazer is Mannhardt's disciple. But where, all this time, is there a reference by Mannhardt to 'the general principles of comparative philology'? Where does he accept 'the omnipresent Sun and the inevitable Dawn'? Why, he says the reverse; he says in this letter that he is immeasurably removed from accepting them at all as Mr. Max Müller accepts them!

'I am very far from looking upon all myths as psychical reflections of physical phenomena, still less as of exclusively solar or meteorological phenomena, like Kuhn, Schwartz, Max Müller and their school.' What a queer way of expressing his agreement with Mr. Max Müller!

The Professor expostulates with Mannhardt (1. xx.):—'Where has any one of us ever done this?' Well, when Mannhardt said 'all myths,' he wrote colloquially. Shall we say that he meant 'most myths,' 'a good many myths,' 'a myth or two here and there'? Whatever he meant, he meant that he was 'still more than very far removed from looking upon all myths' as Mr. Max Müller does.

Mannhardt's next passage I quote entire and textually from Mr. Max Müller's translation:—

I have learnt to appreciate poetical and literary production as an essential element in the development of mythology, and to draw and utilise the consequences arising from this state of things. [Who has not?] But, on the other hand, I hold it as quite certain that a portion of the older myths arose from nature poetry which is no longer directly intelligible to us, but has to be interpreted by means of analogies. Nor does it follow that these

29

myths betray any historical identity; they only testify to the same kind of conception and tendency prevailing on similar stages of development. Of these nature myths some have reference to the life and the circumstances of the sun, and our first steps towards an understanding of them are helped on by such nature poetry as the Lettish, which has not yet been obscured by artistic and poetical reflexion. In that poetry mythical personalities confessedly belonging to a solar sphere are transferred to a large number of poetical representatives, of which the explanation must consequently be found in the same (solar) sphere of nature. My method here is just the same as that applied by me to the Tree-cult.'

Mr. Max Müller asks, 'Where is there any difference between this, the latest and final system adopted by Mannhardt, and my own system which I put forward in 1856?' (1. xxi.)

How Mannhardt differs from Mr. Max Müller

I propose to show wherein the difference lies. Mannhardt says, 'My method is just the same as that applied by me to the Tree-cult.' What was that method?

Mannhardt, in the letter quoted by Mr. Max Müller, goes on to describe it; but Mr. Max Müller omits the description, probably not realising its importance. For Mannhardt's method is the reverse of that practised under the old colours to which he is said to have returned.

Mannhardt's Method

'My method is here the same as in the Tree-cult. I start from a given collection of facts, of which the central idea is distinct and generally admitted, and consequently offers a firm basis for explanation. I illustrate from this and from well-founded analogies. Continuing from these, I seek to elucidate darker things. I search out the simplest radical ideas and perceptions, the germ-cells from whose combined growth mythical tales form themselves in very different ways.'

Mr. Frazer gives us a similar description of Mannhardt's method, whether dealing with sun myths or tree myths.[51] 'Mannhardt set himself systematically to collect, compare, and explain the living superstitions of the peasantry.' Now Mr. Max

---

[51] Golden Bough, 1. ix.

Müller has just confessed, as a reason for incompetence to criticise Mannhardt's labours, 'my want of knowledge of the materials with which he dealt—the popular customs and traditions of Germany.' And yet he asks where there is any difference between his system and Mannhardt's. Mannhardt's is the study of rural survival, the system of folklore. Mr. Max Müller's is the system of comparative philology about which in this place Mannhardt does not say one single word. Mannhardt interprets some myths 'arising from nature poetry, no longer intelligible to us,' by analogies; Mr. Max Müller interprets them by etymologies.

The difference is incalculable; not that Mannhardt always abstains from etymologising.

Another Claim on Mannhardt

While maintaining that 'all comparative mythology must rest on comparison of names as its most certain basis' (a system which Mannhardt declares explicitly to be so far 'a failure'), Mr. Max Müller says, 'It is well known that in his last, nay posthumous essay, Mannhardt, no mean authority, returned to the same conviction.' I do not know which is Mannhardt's very last essay, but I shall prove that in the posthumous essays Mannhardt threw cold water on the whole method of philological comparative mythology.

However, as proof of Mannhardt's return to Mr. Max Müller's convictions, our author cites Mythologische Forschungen (pp. 86-113).

What Mannhardt said

In the passages here produced as proof of Mannhardt's conversion, he is not investigating a myth at all, or a name which occurs in mythology. He is trying to discover the meaning of the practices of the Lupercalia at Rome. In February, says Dionysius of Halicarnassus, the Romans held a popular festival, and lads ran round naked, save for skins of victims, whipping the spectators. Mannhardt, in his usual way, collects all the facts first, and then analyses the name Luperci. This does not make him a philological mythologist. To take a case in point, at Selkirk and Queensferry the bounds are ridden, or walked, by 'Burleymen' or 'Burrymen.'[52] After examining the facts we examine the words, and ask, 'Why Burley or Burry men?' At Queensferry, by a folk etymology, one of the lads wears a coat stuck over with burrs. But 'Borough-men' seems the

_____

[52] περιελθεῖν δρόμῳ τὴν κώμην. Dionys. i. 80.

31

probable etymology. As we examine the names Burley, or Burry men, so Mannhardt examines the name Luperci; and if a true etymology can be discovered, it will illustrate the original intention of the Lupercalia (p. 86).

He would like to explain the Lupercalia as a popular play, representing the spirits of vegetation opposing the spirits of infertility. 'But we do not forget that our whole theory of the development of the rite rests on a hypothesis which the lack of materials prevents us from demonstrating.' He would explain Luperci as Lupiherci—'wolf-goats.' Over this we need not linger; but how does all this prove Mannhardt to have returned to the method of comparing Greek with Vedic divine names, and arriving thence at some celestial phenomenon as the basis of a terrestrial myth? Yet he sometimes does this.

My Relations to Mannhardt

If anything could touch and move an unawakened anthropologist it would be the conversion of Mannhardt. My own relations with his ideas have the interest of illustrating mental coincidences. His name does not occur, I think, in the essay, 'The Method of Folklore,' in the first edition of my Custom and Myth. In that essay I take, as an example of the method, the Scottish and Northumbrian Kernababy, the puppet made out of the last gleanings of harvest. This I compared to the Greek Demeter of the harvest-home, with sheaves and poppies in her hands, in the immortal Seventh Idyll of Theocritus. Our Kernababy, I said, is a stunted survival of our older 'Maiden,' 'a regular image of the harvest goddess,' and I compared κορη. Next I gave the parallel case from ancient Peru, and the odd accidental coincidence that there the maize was styled Mama Cora (μητηρ κορη!).

In entire ignorance of Mannhardt's corn-spirit, or corn-mother, I was following Mannhardt's track. Indeed, Mr. Max Müller has somewhere remarked that I popularise Mannhardt's ideas. Naturally he could not guess that the coincidence was accidental and also inevitable. Two men, unknown to each other, were using the same method on the same facts.

Mannhardt's Return to his old Colours

If, then, Mannhardt was re-converted, it would be a potent argument for my conversion. But one is reminded of the re-conversion of Prince Charles. In 1750 he 'deserted the errors of the

32

Church of Rome for those of the Church of England.' Later he returned, or affected to return, to the ancient faith.

A certain Cardinal seemed contented therewith, and, as the historian remarks, 'was clearly a man not difficult to please.' Mr. Max Müller reminds me of the good Cardinal. I do not feel so satisfied as he does of Mannhardt's re-conversion.

Mannhardt's Attitude to Philology

We have heard Mannhardt, in a letter partly cited by Mr. Max Müller, describe his own method. He begins with what is certain and intelligible, a mass of popular customs. These he explains by analogies. He passes from the known to the obscure. Philological mythologists begin with the unknown, the name of a god. This they analyse, extract a meaning, and (proceeding to the known) fit the facts of the god's legend into the sense of his name. The methods are each other's opposites, yet the letter in which Mannhardt illustrates this fact is cited as a proof of his return to his old colours.

Irritating Conduct of Mannhardt

Nothing irritates philological mythologists so much, nothing has injured them so much in the esteem of the public which 'goes into these things a little,' as the statement that their competing etymologies and discrepant interpretations of mythical names are mutually destructive. I have been told that this is 'a mean argument.' But if one chemical analyst found bismuth where another found iridium, and a third found argon, the public would begin to look on chemistry without enthusiasm; still more so if one chemist rarely found anything but inevitable bismuth or omnipresent iridium. Now Mannhardt uses this 'mean argument.'

Mannhardt on Demeter Erinnys

In a posthumous work, Mythologische Forschungen (1884), the work from which Mr. Max Müller cites the letter to Müllenhoff, Mannhardt discusses Demeter Erinnys. She is the Arcadian goddess, who, in the form of a mare, became mother of Despoina and the horse Arion, by Poseidon.[53] Her anger at the unhandsome behaviour of Poseidon caused Demeter to be called Erinnys—'to be angry' being εριννειν in Arcadian—a folk-etymology, clearly.

---

[53] Pausanias, viii. 25.

Mannhardt first dives deep into the sources for this fable.[54] Arion, he decides, is no mythological personification, but a poetical ideal (Bezeichnung) of the war-horse. Legend is ransacked for proof of this. Poseidon is the lord of wind and wave. Now, there are waves of corn, under the wind, as well as waves of the sea. When the Suabian rustic sees the wave running over the corn, he says, Da lauft das Pferd, and Greeks before Homer would say, in face of the billowing corn, Ἐκιθι θεουσι ιπποι, There run horses! And Homer himself[55] says that the horses of Erichthonius, children of Boreas, ran over cornfield and sea. We ourselves speak of sea-waves as 'white horses.' So, to be brief, Mannhardt explains the myth of Demeter Erinnys becoming, as a mare, a mother by Poseidon as a horse, thus, 'Poseidon Hippies, or Poseidon in horse's form, rushes through the growing grain and weds Demeter,' and he cites peasant proverbs, such as Das Korn heirathet; das Korn feiert Hochzeit (p. 264). 'This is the germ of the Arcadian Saga.'

> *The Arcadian myth of Demeter Erinnys is undeniably a blending of the epic tradition [of the ideal war-horse] with the local cult of Demeter. . . . It is a probable hypothesis that the belief in the wedding of Demeter and Poseidon comes from the sight of the waves passing over the cornfield. . . .'*[56]

It is very neat! But a certain myth of Loki in horse-form comes into memory, and makes me wonder how Mannhardt would have dealt with that too liberal narrative.

Loki, as a mare (he being a male god), became, by the horse of a giant, the father of Sleipnir, Odin's eight-footed steed. Mr. W. A. Craigie supplies this note on Loki's analogy with Poseidon, as a horse, in the waves of corn:—

> *'In North Jutland, when the vapours are seen going with a wavy motion along the earth in the heat of summer, they say, "Loki is sowing oats today," or "Loki is driving his goats."*
>
> *'N.B.—Oats in Danish are havre, which suggests O.N. hafrar, goats. Modern Icelandic has hafrar=oats, but the word is not found in the old language.'*

Is Loki a corn-spirit?

---

54 Myth. Forsch. p. 244.
55 Iliad, xx. 226.
56 Myth. Forsch, p. 265.

Mannhardt's 'Mean Argument'

Mannhardt now examines the explanations of Demeter Erinnys, and her legend, given by Preller, E. Curtius, O. Müller, A. Kuhn, W. Sonne, Max Müller, E. Burnouf, de Gubernatis, Schwartz, and H. D. Müller. 'Here,' he cries, 'is a variegated list of hypotheses!' Demeter is

> Storm-cloud
> Sun Goddess
> Earth and Moon Goddess
> Dawn
> Night.

Poseidon is

> Sea
> Storm God
> Cloud-hidden Sun
> Rain God.

Despoina is

> Rain
> Thunder
> Moon.

Arion, the horse, is

> Lightning
> Sun
> Thunder-horse.

Erinnys is

> Storm-cloud
> Red Dawn.

Mannhardt decides, after this exhibition of guesses, that the Demeter legends cannot be explained as refractions of any natural phenomena in the heavens (p. 275). He concludes that the myth of Demeter Erinnys, and the parallel Vedic story of Saranyu (who also had an amour as a mare), are 'incongruous,' and that neither sheds any light on the other. He protests against the whole tendency to find prototypes of all Aryan myths in the Veda, and to think that, with a few exceptions, all mythology is a terrestrial reflection of celestial phenomena (p. 280). He then goes into the contending etymologies of Demeter, and decides ('for the man was mortal and had been a' philologer) in favour of his own guess, Ζεια δη+μητηρ='Corn-mother' (p. 294).

This essay on Demeter was written by Mannhardt in the summer of 1877, a year after the letter which is given as evidence that he had 'returned to his old colours.' The essay shows him using the philological string of 'variegated hypotheses' as anything but an argument in favour of the philological method. On the other hand, he warns us against the habit, so common in the philological school, of looking for prototypes of all Aryan myths in the Veda, and of finding in most myths a reflection on earth of phenomena in the heavens, Erinnys being either Storm-cloud or Dawn, according to the taste and fancy of the inquirer. We also find Mannhardt, in 1877, starting from the known—legend and rural survival in phrase and custom—and so advancing to the unknown—the name Demeter. The philologists commence with the unknown, the old name, Demeter Erinnys, explain it to taste, and bring the legend into harmony with their explanation. I cannot say, then, that I share Mr. Max Müller's impression. I do not feel sure that Mannhardt did return to his old colours.

Why Mannhardt is Thought to have been Converted

Mannhardt's friend, Müllenhoff, had an aversion to solar myths. He said:[57] 'I deeply mistrust all these combinations of the new so-called comparative mythology.' Mannhardt was preparing to study Lithuanian solar myths, based on Lithuanian and Lettish marriage songs. Müllenhoff and Scherer seem to have thought this work too solar for their taste. Mannhardt therefore replied to their objections in the letter quoted in part by Mr. Max Müller. Mannhardt was not the man to neglect or suppress solar myths when he found them, merely because he did not believe that a great many other myths which had been claimed as celestial were solar. Like every sensible person, he knew that there are numerous real, obvious, confessed solar myths not derived from a disease of language. These arise from (1) the impulse to account for the doings of the Sun by telling a story about him as if he were a person; (2) from the natural poetry of the human mind.[58] What we think they are not shown to arise from is forgetfulness of meanings of old words, which, ex hypothesi, have become proper names.

That is the theory of the philological school, and to that theory, to these colours, I see no proof (in the evidence given) that

---

[57] September 19, 1875. Myth. Forsch. xiv.
[58] For undeniable solar myths see M. R. R. i. 124-135.

Mannhardt had returned. But 'the scalded child dreads cold water,' and Müllenhoff apparently dreaded even real solar myths. Mr. Max Müller, on the other hand (if I do not misinterpret him), supposes that Mannhardt had returned to the philological method, partly because he was interested in real solar myths and in the natural poetry of illiterate races.

Mannhardt's Final Confession

Mannhardt's last work published in his life days was Antike Wald- und Feldkulte (1877). In the preface, dated November 1, 1876 (after the famous letter of May 1876), he explains the growth of his views and criticises his predecessors. After doing justice to Kuhn and his comparisons of European with Indian myths, he says that, in his opinion, comparative Indo-Germanic mythology has not yet borne the expected fruits. 'The assured gains shrink into very few divine names, such as Dyaus—Zeus—Tius, Parjany—Perkunas, Bhaga—Bug, Varuna—Uranus, &c.' I wish he had completed the list included in &c. Other equations, as Sarameya=Hermeias, Saranyu=Demeter Erinnys, he fears will not stand close criticism. He dreads that jeux d'esprit (geistvolle Spiele des Witzes) may once more encroach on science. Then, after a lucid statement of Mr. Max Müller's position, he says, 'Ich vermag dem von M. Müller aufgestellten Principe, wenn überhaupt eine, so doch nur eine sehr beschrankte Geltung zuzugestehen.'

'To the principle of Max Müller I can only assign a very limited value, if any value at all.'[59]

'Taken all in all, I consider the greater part of the results hitherto obtained in the field of Indo-Germanic comparative mythology to be, as yet, a failure, premature or incomplete, my own efforts in German Myths (1858) included. That I do not, however, "throw out the babe with the bath," as the proverb goes, my essay on Lettish sun myths in Bastian-Hartmann's Ethnological Journal will bear witness.'

Such is Mannhardt's conclusion. Taken in connection with his still later essay on Demeter, it really leaves no room for doubt. There, I think, he does 'throw out the child with the bath,' throw the knife after the handle. I do not suppose that Mr. Max Müller ever did quote Mannhardt as one of his supporters, but such a claim, if really made, would obviously give room for criticism.

---

[59] Op. cit. p. xx.

Mannhardt on Solar Myths

What the attitude of Mannhardt was, in 1877 and later, we have seen. He disbelieves in the philological system of explaining myths by etymological conjectures. He disbelieves in the habit of finding, in myths of terrestrial occurrences, reflections of celestial phenomena. But earlier, in his long essay Die lettischen Sonnenmythen (in Zeitschrift für Ethnologie, 1875), he examines the Lettish popular songs about the Sun, the Sun's daughters, the god-sons, and so forth. Here, of course, he is dealing with popular songs explicitly devoted to solar phenomena, in their poetical aspect. In the Lettish Sun-songs and Sun-myths of the peasants we see, he says, a myth-world 'in process of becoming,' in an early state of development, as in the Veda (p. 325). But, we may reply, in the Veda, myths are already full-grown, or even decadent. Already there are unbelievers in the myths. Thus we would say, in the Veda we have (1) myths of nature, formed in the remote past, and (2) poetical phrases about heavenly phenomena, which resemble the nature-poetry of the Letts, but which do not become full-grown myths. The Lett songs, also, have not developed into myths, of which (as in the Apollo and Daphne story, by Mr. Max Müller's hypothesis) the original meaning is lost.

In the Lett songs we have a mass of nature-pictures—the boat and the apples of the Sun, the red cloak hung on the oak-tree, and so on; pictures by which it is sought to make elemental phenomena intelligible, by comparison with familiar things. Behind the phenomena are, in popular belief, personages—mythical personages—the Sun as 'a magnified non-natural man,' or woman; the Sun's mother, daughters, and other heavenly people. Their conduct is 'motived' in a human way. Stories are told about them: the Sun kills the Moon, who revives.

All this is perfectly familiar everywhere. Savages, in their fables, account for solar, lunar, and similar elemental processes, on the theory that the heavenly bodies are, and act like, human beings. The Eskimo myth of the spots on the Moon, marks of ashes thrown by the Sun in a love-quarrel, is an excellent example. But in all this there is no 'disease of language.' These are frank nature-myths, 'ætiological,' giving a fabulous reason for facts of nature.

Mannhardt on Märchen

But Mannhardt goes farther. He not only recognises, as everyone must do, the Sun, as explicitly named, when he plays his part in myth, or popular tale (Märchen). He thinks that even when the Sun is not named, his presence, and reference to him, and derivation of the incidents in Märchen from solar myth, may sometimes be detected with great probability (pp. 326, 327). But he adds, 'not that every Märchen contains a reference to Nature; that I am far from asserting' (p. 327).

Now perhaps nobody will deny that some incidents in Märchen may have been originally suggested by nature-myths. The all-swallowing and all-disgorging beast, wolf, or ogre, may have been derived from a view of Night as the all-swallower. But to disengage natural phenomena, mythically stated, from the human tangle of Märchen, to find natural phenomena in such a palimpsest as Perrault's courtly and artificial version of a French popular tale, is a delicate and dangerous task. In many stories a girl has three balls—one of silver, one of gold, one of diamond—which she offers, in succession, as bribes. This is a perfectly natural invention. It is perilous to connect these balls, gifts of ascending value, with the solar apple of iron, silver, and gold (p. 103 and note 5). It is perilous, and it is quite unnecessary. Some one—Gubernatis, I think—has explained the naked sword of Aladdin, laid between him and the Sultan's daughter in bed, as the silver sickle of the Moon. Really the sword has an obvious purpose and meaning, and is used as a symbol in proxy-marriages. The blood shed by Achilles in his latest victories is elsewhere explained as red clouds round the setting Sun, which is conspicuously childish. Mannhardt leans, at least, in this direction.

'The Two Brothers'

Mannhardt takes the old Egyptian tale of 'The Two Brothers,' Bitiou and Anepou. This fable, as old, in actual written literature, as Moses, is a complex of half the Märchen plots and incidents in the world. It opens with the formula of Potiphar's Wife. The falsely accused brother flies, and secretes his life, or separable soul, in a flower of the mystic Vale of Acacias. This affair of the separable soul may be studied in Mr. Hartland's Perseus, and it animates, as we shall see, Mr. Frazer's theory of the Origin of Totemism. A golden lock of the wicked wife's hair is then borne by the Nile to the king's palace in Egypt. He will insist on marrying the lady of the lock. Here we are in the Cinderella formula, en plein, which may be studied, in African and Santhal shapes, in Miss Coxe's valuable Cinderella.[60] Pharaoh's wise men decide that the owner of the lock of hair is (like Egyptian royalty at large) a daughter of the Sun-god

---

[60] Folk Lore Society.

(p. 239). Here is the Sun, in all his glory; but here we are dealing with a literary version of the Märchen, accommodated to royal tastes and Egyptian ideas of royalty by a royal scribe, the courtly Perrault of the Egyptian Roi-Soleil. Who can say what he introduced?—while we can say that the Sun-god is absent in South African and Santhal and other variants. The Sun may have slipped out here, may have been slipped in there; the faintest glimmer of the historical sense prevents us from dogmatising.

Wedded to Pharaoh, the wicked wife, pursuing her vengeance on Bitiou, cuts down his life-tree. Anepou, his brother, however, recovers his concealed heart (life), and puts it in water. Bitiou revives. He changes himself into the sacred Bull, Apis—a feature in the story which is practically possible in Egypt alone. The Bull tells the king his story, but the wicked wife has the Bull slain, as by Cambyses in Herodotus. Two of his blood-drops become two persea trees. One of them confesses the fact to the wicked wife. She has them cut down; a chip flies into her mouth, she becomes a mother by the chip, the boy (Bitiou) again becomes king, and slays his mother, the wicked wife.

In the tree, any tree, acacia or persea, Mannhardt wishes to recognise the Sun-tree of the Lett songs. The red blossoms of the persea tree are a symbol of the Sun-tree: of Horus. He compares features, not always very closely analogous, in European Märchen. For example, a girl hides in a tree, like Charles II. at Boscobel. That is not really analogous with Bitiou's separable life in the acacia! 'Anepou' is like 'Anapu,' Anubis. The Bull is the Sun, is Osiris—dead in winter. Mr. Frazer, Mannhardt's disciple, protests à grands cris against these identifications when made by others than Mannhardt, who says, 'The Märchen is an old obscure solar myth' (p. 242). To others the story of Bitiou seems an Egyptian literary complex, based on a popular set of tales illustrating furens quid femina possit, and illustrating the world-wide theory of the separable life, dragging in formulas from other Märchen, and giving to all a thoroughly classical Egyptian colouring.[61] Solar myths, we think, have not necessarily anything to make in the matter.

The Golden Fleece

Mannhardt reasons in much the same way about the Golden Fleece. This is a peculiarly Greek feature, interwoven with the world-wide Märchen of the Lad, the Giant's helpful daughter, her

---

[61] Von einem der vorzüglichsten Schiriftgelehrten, Annana, in klassischer Darstellung aufgezeichneten Märchens, p. 240.

aid in accomplishing feats otherwise impossible, and the pursuit of the pair by the father. I have studied the story—as it occurs in Samoa, among Red Indian tribes, and elsewhere—in 'A Far-travelled Tale.'[62] In our late Greek versions the Quest of the Fleece of Gold occurs, but in no other variants known to me. There is a lamb (a boy changed into a lamb) in Romaic. His fleece is of no interest to anybody. Out of his body grows a tree with a golden apple. Sun-yarns occur in popular songs. Mannhardt (pp. 282, 283) abounds in solar explanations of the Fleece of Gold, hanging on the oak-tree in the dark Ææan forest. Idyia, wife of the Colchian king, 'is clearly the Dawn.' Aia is the isle of the Sun. Helle=Surya, a Sanskrit Sun-goddess; the golden ram off whose back she falls, while her brother keeps his seat, is the Sun. Her brother, Phrixus, may be the Daylight. The oak-tree in Colchis is the Sun-tree of the Lettish songs. Perseus is a hero of Light, born in the Dark Tower (Night) from the shower of gold (Sun-rays).

'We can but say "it may be so,"' but who could explain all the complex Perseus-saga as a statement about elemental phenomena? Or how can the Far-travelled Tale of the Lad and the Giant's Daughter be interpreted to the same effect, above all in the countless examples where no Fleece of Gold occurs? The Greek tale of Jason is made up of several Märchen, as is the Odyssey, by epic poets. These Märchen have no necessary connection with each other; they are tagged on to each other, and localised in Greece and on the Euxine.[63] A poetic popular view of the Sun may have lent the peculiar, and elsewhere absent, incident of the quest of the Fleece of Gold on the shores of the Black Sea. The old epic poets may have borrowed from popular songs like the Lettish chants (p. 328). A similar dubious adhesion may be given by us in the case of Castor and Polydeuces (Morning and Evening Stars?), and Helen (Dawn),[64] and the Hesperides (p. 234). The germs of the myths may be popular poetical views of elemental phenomena. But to insist on elemental allegories through all the legends of the Dioskouroi, and of the Trojan war, would be to strain a hypothesis beyond the breaking-point. Much, very much, is epic invention, unverkennbar das werk der Dichter (p. 328).

Mannhardt's Approach to Mr. Max Müller

In this essay on Lettish Sun-songs (1875) Mannhardt comes

---

[62] Custom and Myth.
[63] See Preface to Mrs. Hunt's translation of Grimm's Märchen.
[64] P. 309.

nearest to Mr. Max Müller. He cites passages from him with approval (cf. pp. 314, 322). His explanations, by aid of Sun-songs, of certain features in Greek mythology are plausible, and may be correct. But we turn to Mannhardt's explicit later statement of his own position in 1877, and to his posthumous essays, published in 1884; and, on the whole, we find, in my opinion, much more difference from than agreement with the Oxford Professor, whose Dawn-Daphne and other equations Mannhardt dismisses, and to whose general results (in mythology) he assigns a value so restricted. It is a popular delusion that the anthropological mythologists deny the existence of solar myths, or of nature-myths in general. These are extremely common. What we demur to is the explanation of divine and heroic myths at large as solar or elemental, when the original sense has been lost by the ancient narrators, and when the elemental explanation rests on conjectural and conflicting etymologies and interpretations of old proper names—Athene, Hera, Artemis, and the rest. Nevertheless, while Mannhardt, in his works on Tree-cult, and on Field and Wood Cult, and on the 'Corn Demon,' has wandered far from 'his old colours'— while in his posthumous essays he is even more of a deserter, his essay on Lettish Sun-myths shows an undeniable tendency to return to Mr. Max Müller's camp. This was what made his friends so anxious. It is probably wisest to form our opinion of his final attitude on his preface to his last book published in his life-time. In that the old colours are not exactly his chosen banner; nor can the flag of the philological school be inscribed tandem triumphans.

In brief, Mannhardt's return to his old colours (1875-76) seems to have been made in a mood from which he again later passed away. But either modern school of mythology may cite him as an ally in one or other of his phases of opinion.

PHILOLOGY AND DEMETER ERINNYS

Mr. Max Müller on Demeter Erinnys

Like Mannhardt, our author in his new treatise discusses the strange old Arcadian myth of the horse-Demeter Erinnys (ii. 537). He tells the unseemly tale, and asks why the Earth goddess became a mare? Then he gives the analogous myth from the Rig-Veda,[65] which, as it stands, is 'quite unintelligible.' But Yâska explains that Saranyu, daughter of Tvashtri, in the form of a mare, had twins by Vivasvat, in the shape of a stallion. Their offspring were the Asvins, who are more or less analogous in their helpful character to Castor and Pollux. Now, can it be by accident that Saranyu in the Veda is Erinnys in Greek? To this 'equation,' as we saw, Mannhardt demurred in 1877. Who was Saranyu? Yâska says 'the Night;' that was Yâska's idea. Mr. Max Müller adds, 'I think he is right,' and that Saranyu is 'the grey dawn' (ii. 541).

'But,' the bewildered reader exclaims, 'Dawn is one thing and Night is quite another.' So Yâska himself was intelligent enough to observe, 'Night is the wife of Aditya; she vanishes at sunrise.' However, Night in Mr. Max Müller's system 'has just got to be' Dawn, a position proved thus: 'Yâska makes this clear by saying that the time of the Asvins, sons of Saranyu, is after midnight,' but that 'when darkness prevails over light, that is Madhyama; when light prevails over darkness, that is Aditya,' both being Asvins. They (the Asvins) are, in fact, darkness and light; and therefore, I understand, Saranyu, who is Night, and not an Asvin at all, is Dawn! To make this perfectly clear, remember that the husband of Saranyu, whom she leaves at sunrise, is—I give you three guesses—is the Sun! The Sun's wife leaves the Sun at sunrise.[66] This is proved, for Aditya is Vivasvat=the Sun, and is the husband of Saranyu (ii. 541). These methods of proving Night to be Dawn, while the substitute for both in the bed of the Sun 'may have been meant for the gloaming' (ii. 542), do seem to be geistvolle Spiele des Witzes, ingenious jeux d'esprit, as Mannhardt says, rather than logical arguments.

But we still do not know how the horse and mare came in, or why the statue of Demeter had a horse's head. 'This seems simply to be due to the fact that, quite apart from this myth, the sun had, in India at least, often been conceived as a horse . . . . and the dawn

---

[65] x. 17. Cf. Muir, Sanskrit Texts, v. 277.
[66]

had been likened to a mare.' But how does this explain the problem? The Vedic poets cited (ii. 542) either referred to the myth which we have to explain, or they used a poetical expression, knowing perfectly well what they meant. As long as they knew what they meant, they could not make an unseemly fable out of a poetical phrase. Not till after the meaning was forgotten could the myth arise. But the myth existed already in the Veda! And the unseemliness is precisely what we have to account for; that is our enigma.

Once more, Demeter is a goddess of Earth, not of Dawn. How, then, does the explanation of a hypothetical Dawn-myth apply to the Earth? Well, perhaps the story, the unseemly story, was first told of Erinnys (who also is 'the inevitable Dawn') or of Deo, 'and this name of Deo, or Dyâvâ, was mixed up with a hypokoristic form of Demeter, Deo, and thus led to the transference of her story to Demeter. I know this will sound very unlikely to Greek scholars, yet I see no other way out of our difficulties' (ii. 545). Phonetic explanations follow.

'To my mind,' says our author, 'there is no chapter in mythology in which we can so clearly read the transition of an auroral myth of the Veda into an epic chapter of Greece as in the chapter of Saranyu (or Suramâ) and the Asvins, ending in the chapter of Helena and her brothers, the Διοσκοροι λευκοπωλοι' (ii. 642). Here, as regards the Asvins and the Dioskouroi, Mannhardt may be regarded as Mr. Max Müller's ally; but compare his note, A. F. u. W. K. p. xx.

My Theory of the Horse Demeter

Mannhardt, I think, ought to have tried at an explanation of myths so closely analogous as those two, one Indian, one Greek, in which a goddess, in the shape of a mare, becomes mother of twins by a god in the form of a stallion. As Mr. Max Müller well says, 'If we look about for analogies we find nothing, as far as I know, corresponding to the well-marked features of this barbarous myth among any of the uncivilised tribes of the earth. If we did, how we should rejoice! Why, then, should we not rejoice when we find the allusion in Rig Veda?' (x 17, 1).

I do rejoice! The 'song of triumph,' as Professor Tiele says, will be found in M. R. R. ii. 266 (note), where I give the Vedic and other references. I even asked why Mr. Max Müller did not produce this proof of the identity of Saranyu and Demeter Erinnys in his Selected Essays (pp. 401, 492).

I cannot explain why this tale was told both of Erinnys and of

44

Saranyu.   Granting the certainty of the etymological equation, Saranyu=Erinnys (which Mannhardt doubted), the chances against fortuitous coincidence may be reckoned by algebra, and Mr. Edgeworth's trillions of trillions feebly express it.   Two goddesses, Indian and Greek, have, ex hypothesi, the same name, and both, as mares, are mothers of twins.   Though the twins (in India the Asvins, in Greek an ideal war-horse and a girl) differ in character, still the coincidence is evidential.   Explain it I cannot, and, clearly as the confession may prove my lack of scientific exactness, I make it candidly.

If I must offer a guess, it is that Greeks, and Indians of India, inherited a very ordinary savage idea.   The gods in savage myths are usually beasts.   As beasts they beget anthropomorphic offspring.   This is the regular rule in totemism.   In savage myths we are not told 'a god' (Apollo, or Zeus, or Poseidon) 'put on beast shape and begat human sons and daughters' (Helen, the Telmisseis, and so on).   The god in savage myths was a beast already, though he could, of course, shift shapes like any 'medicine-man,' or modern witch who becomes a hare.   This is not the exception but the rule in savage mythology.   Anyone can consult my Myth, Ritual, and Religion, or Mr. Frazer's work Totemism, for abundance of evidence.   To Loki, a male god, prosecuting his amours as a female horse, I have already alluded, and in M. R. R. give cases from the Satapatha Brahmana.

The Saranyu-Erinnys myth dates, I presume, from this savage state of fancy; but why the story occurred both in Greece and India, I protest that I cannot pretend to explain, except on the hypothesis that the ancestors of Greek and Vedic peoples once dwelt together, had a common stock of savage fables, and a common or kindred language.   After their dispersion, the fables admitted discrepancies, as stories in oral circulation occasionally do.   This is the only conjecture which I feel justified in suggesting to account for the resemblances and incongruities between the myths of the mare Demeter-Erinnys and the mare Saranyu.

TOTEMISM

Totemism

To the strange and widely diffused institution of 'Totemism' our author often returns. I shall deal here with his collected remarks on the theme, the more gladly as the treatment shows how very far Mr. Max Müller is from acting with a shadow of unfairness when he does not refer to special passages in his opponent's books. He treats himself and his own earlier works in the same fashion, thereby, perhaps, weakening his argument, but also demonstrating his candour, were any such demonstration required.

On totems he opens (i. 7)—

'When we come to special cases we must not imagine that much can be gained by using such general terms as Animism, Totemism, Fetishism, &c., as solvents of mythological problems. To my mind, all such general terms, not excluding even Darwinism or Puseyism, seem most objectionable, because they encourage vague thought, vague praise, or vague blame.

'It is, for instance, quite possible to place all worship of animal gods, all avoidance of certain kinds of animal food, all adoption of animal names as the names of men and families, under the wide and capacious cover of totemism. All theriolatry would thus be traced back to totemism. I am not aware, however, that any Egyptologists have adopted such a view to account for the animal forms of the Egyptian gods. Sanskrit scholars would certainly hesitate before seeing in Indra a totem because he is called vrishabha, or bull, or before attempting to explain on this ground the abstaining from beef on the part of orthodox Hindus [i. 7].'

Totemism Defined

I think I have defined totemism,[67] and the reader may consult Mr. Frazer's work on the subject, or Mr. MacLennan's essays, or 'Totemism' in the Encyclopædia Britannica. However, I shall define totemism once more. It is a state of society and cult, found most fully developed in Australia and North America, in which sets of persons, believing themselves to be akin by blood, call each such set by the name of some plant, beast, or other class of objects in nature. One kin may be wolves, another bears, another cranes, and so on.

---

[67] M. R. R. i. 58-81.

Each kin derives its kin-name from its beast, plant, or what not; pays to it more or less respect, usually abstains from killing, eating, or using it (except in occasional sacrifices); is apt to claim descent from or relationship with it, and sometimes uses its effigy on memorial pillars, carved pillars outside huts, tattooed on the skin, and perhaps in other ways not known to me. In Australia and North America, where rules are strict, a man may not marry a woman of his own totem; and kinship is counted through mothers in many, but not in all, cases. Where all these notes are combined we have totemism. It is plain that two or three notes of it may survive where the others have perished; may survive in ritual and sacrifice,[68] and in bestial or semi-bestial gods of certain nomes, or districts, in ancient Egypt;[69] in Pictish names;[70] in claims of descent from beasts, or gods in the shape of beasts; in the animals sacred to gods, as Apollo or Artemis, and so on. Such survivals are possible enough in evolution, but the evidence needs careful examination. Animal attributes and symbols and names in religion are not necessarily totemistic. Mr. Max Müller asks if 'any Egyptologists have adopted' the totem theory. He is apparently oblivious of Professor Sayce's reference to a prehistoric age, 'when the religious creed of Egypt was still totemism.'

Dr. Codrington is next cited for the apparent absence of totemism in the Solomon Islands and Polynesia, and Professor Oldenberg as denying that 'animal names of persons and clans [necessarily?] imply totemism.' Who says that they do? 'Clan Chattan,' with its cat crest, may be based, not on a totem, but on a popular etymology. Animal names of individuals have nothing to do with totems. A man has no business to write on totemism if he does not know these facts.

What a Totem is

Though our adversary now abandons totems, he returns to them elsewhere (i. 198-202). 'Totem is the corruption of a term used by North American Indians in the sense of clan-mark or sign-board ("ododam").' The totem was originally a rude emblem of an animal or other object 'placed by North American Indians in front of their settlements.'

---

[68] See Robertson Smith on 'Semitic Religion.'
[69] See Sayce's Herodotus, p. 344.
[70] See Rhys' Rhind Lectures; I am not convinced by the evidence.

The Evidence for Sign-boards

Our author's evidence for sign-boards is from an Ottawa Indian, and is published from his MS. by Mr. Hoskyns Abrahall.[71] The testimony is of the greatest merit, for it appears to have first seen the light in a Canadian paper of 1858. Now in 1858 totems were only spoken of in Lafitau, Long, and such old writers, and in Cooper's novels. They had not become subjects of scientific dispute, so the evidence is uncontaminated by theory. The Indians were, we learn, divided into [local?] tribes, and these 'into sections or families according to their ododams'—devices, signs, in modern usage 'coats of arms.' [Perhaps 'crests' would be a better word.] All people of one ododam (apparently under male kinship) lived together in a special section of each village. At the entrance to the enclosure was the figure of an animal, or some other sign, set up on the top of one of the posts. Thus everybody knew what family dwelt in what section of the village. Some of the families were called after their ododam. But the family with the bear ododam were called Big Feet, not Bears. Sometimes parts of different animals were 'quartered' [my suggestion], and one ododam was a small hawk and the fins of a sturgeon.

We cannot tell, of course, on the evidence here, whether 'Big Feet' suggested 'Bear,' or vice versa, or neither. But Mr. Frazer has remarked that periphrases for sacred beasts, like 'Big Feet' for Bear, are not uncommon. Nor can we tell 'what couple of ancestors' a small hawk and a sturgeon's fins represent, unless, perhaps, a hawk and a sturgeon.[72]

For all this, Mr. Max Müller suggests the explanation that people who marked their abode with crow or wolf might come to be called Wolves or Crows.[73] Again, people might borrow beast names from the prevalent beast of their district, as Arkades, Αρκτοι, Bears, and so evolve the myth of descent from Callisto as a she-bear. 'All this, however, is only guesswork.' The Snake Indians worship no snake. [The Snake Indians are not a totem group, but a local tribe named from the Snake River, as we say, 'An Ettrick man.'] Once more, the name-giving beast, say, 'Great Hare,' is explained by Dr. Brinton as 'the inevitable Dawn.'[74] 'Hasty writers,' remarks Dr. Brinton, 'say that the Indians claim descent from different wild beasts.' For evidence I refer to that hasty writer, Mr. Frazer, and his

---

[71] Academy, September 27, 1884.
[72] Anth. Rel. p. 405.
[73] Plantagenet, Planta genista.—A. L.
[74] See M. R. R. ii. 56, for a criticism of this theory.

book, Totemism. For a newly sprung up modern totem our author alludes to a boat, among the Mandans, 'their totem, or tutelary object of worship.' An object of worship, of course, is not necessarily a totem! Nor is a totem by the definition (as a rule one of a class of objects) anything but a natural object. Mr. Max Müller wishes that 'those who write about totems and totemism would tell us exactly what they mean by these words.' I have told him, and indicated better sources. I apply the word totemism to the widely diffused savage institution which I have defined.

More about Totems

The origin of totemism is unknown to me, as to Mr. McLennan and Dr. Robertson Smith, but Mr. Max Müller knows this origin. 'A totem is a clan-mark, then a clan-name, then the name of the ancestor of a clan, and lastly the name of something worshipped by a clan' (i. 201). 'All this applies in the first instance to Red Indians only.' Yes, and 'clan' applies in the first instance to the Scottish clans only! When Mr. Max Müller speaks of 'clans' among the Red Indians, he uses a word whose connotation differs from anything known to exist in America. But the analogy between a Scottish clan and an American totem-kin is close enough to justify Mr. Max Müller in speaking of Red Indian 'clans.' By parity of reasoning, the analogy between the Australian Kobong and the American totem is so complete that we may speak of 'Totemism' in Australia. It would be childish to talk of 'Totemism' in North America, 'Kobongism' in Australia, 'Pacarissaism' in the realm of the Incas: totems, kobongs, and pacarissas all amounting to the same thing, except in one point. I am not aware that Australian blacks erect, or that the subjects of the Incas, or that African and Indian and Asiatic totemists, erected 'sign-boards' anywhere, as the Ottawa writer assures us that the Ottawas do, or used to do. And, if they don't, how do we know that kobongs and pacarissas were developed out of sign-boards?

Heraldry and Totems

The Ottawas are armigeri, are heraldic; so are the natives of Vancouver's Island, who have wooden pillars with elaborate quarterings. Examples are in South Kensington Museum. But this savage heraldry is not nearly so common as the institution of totemism. Thus it is difficult to prove that the heraldry is the origin of totemism, which is just as likely, or more likely, to have been the

49

origin of savage heraldic crests and quarterings. Mr. Max Müller allows that there may be other origins.

Gods and Totems

Our author refers to unnamed writers who call Indra or Ammon a totem (i. 200).

This is a foolish liberty with language. 'Why should not all the gods of Egypt with their heads of bulls and apes and cats be survivals of totemisms?' Why not, indeed? Professor Sayce remarks, 'They were the sacred animals of the clans,' survivals from an age 'when the religion of Egypt was totemism.' 'In Egypt the gods themselves are totem-deities, i.e. personifications or individual representations of the sacred character and attributes which in the purely totem stage of religion were ascribed without distinction to all animals of the holy kind.' So says Dr. Robertson Smith. He and Mr. Sayce are 'scholars,' not mere unscholarly anthropologists.[75]

An Objection

Lastly (ii. 403), when totems infected 'even those who ought to have been proof against this infantile complaint' (which is not even a 'disease of language' of a respectable type), then 'the objection that a totem meant originally a clan-mark was treated as scholastic pedantry.' Alas, I fear with justice! For if I call Mr. Arthur Balfour a Tory will Mr. Max Müller refute my opinion by urging that 'a Tory meant originally an Irish rapparee,' or whatever the word did originally mean?

Mr. Max Müller decides that 'we never find a religion consisting exclusively of a belief in fetishes, or totems, or ancestral spirits.' Here, at last, we are in absolute agreement. So much for totems and sign-boards. Only a weak fanatic will find a totem in every animal connected with gods, sacred names, and religious symbols. But totemism is a fact, whether 'totem' originally meant a clan-mark or sign-board in America or not. And, like Mr. Sayce, Mr. Frazer, Mr. Rhys, Dr. Robertson Smith, I believe that totemism has left marks in civilised myth, ritual, and religion, and that these survivals, not a 'disease of language,' explain certain odd elements in the old civilisations.

---

[75] Religion of the Semites, pp. 208, 209.

Our author's habit of omitting references to his opponents has here caused me infinite inconvenience. He speaks of some eccentric person who has averred that a 'fetish' is a 'totem,' inhabited by 'an ancestral spirit.' To myself it seems that you might as well say 'Abracadabra is gas and gaiters.' As no reference was offered, I invented 'a wild surmise' that Mr. Max Müller had conceivably misapprehended Mr. Frazer's theory of the origin of totems. Had our author only treated himself fairly, he would have referred to his own Anthropological Religion (pp. 126 and 407), where the name of the eccentric definer is given as that of Herr Lippert.[76] Then came into my mind the words of Professor Tiele, 'Beware of weak brethren'—such as Herr Lippert seems, as far as this definition is concerned, to be.

Nobody knows the origin of totemism. We find no race on its way to becoming totemistic, though we find several in the way of ceasing to be so. They are abandoning female kinship for paternity; their rules of marriage and taboo are breaking down; perhaps various totem kindreds of different crests and names are blending into one local tribe, under the name, perhaps, of the most prosperous totem-kin. But we see no race on its way to becoming totemistic, so we have no historical evidence as to the origin of the institution. Mr. McLennan offered no conjecture, Professor Robertson Smith offered none, nor have I displayed the spirit of scientific exactitude by a guess in the dark. To gratify Mr. Max Müller by defining totemism as Mr. McLennan first used the term is all that I dare do. Here one may remark that if Mr. Max Müller really wants 'an accurate definition' of totemism, the works of McLennan, Frazer, Robertson Smith, and myself are accessible, and contain our definitions. He does not produce these definitions, and criticise them; he produces Dr. Lippert's and criticises that. An argument should be met in its strongest and most authoritative form. 'Define what you mean by a totem,' says Professor Max Müller in his Gifford Lectures of 1891 (p. 123). He had to look no further for a definition, an authoritative definition, than to 'totem' in the Encyclopædia Britannica, or to McLennan. Yet his large and intelligent Glasgow audience, and his readers, may very well be under the impression that a definition of 'totem' is 'still to seek,' like Prince Charlie's religion. Controversy simply cannot be profitably conducted on these terms.

'The best representatives of anthropology are now engaged

---

[76] Die Religionen, p. 12.

not so much in comparing as in discriminating.'[77] Why not refer, then, to the results of their discriminating efforts? 'To treat all animal worship as due to totemism is a mistake.' Do we make it?

Mr. Frazer and Myself

There is, or was, a difference of opinion between Mr. Frazer and myself as to the causes of the appearance of certain sacred animals in Greek religion. My notions were published in Myth, Ritual, and Religion (1887), Mr. Frazer's in The Golden Bough (1890). Necessarily I was unaware in 1887 of Mr. Frazer's still unpublished theory. Now that I have read it, he seems to me to have the better logic on his side; and if I do not as yet wholly agree with him, it is because I am not yet certain that both of our theories may not have their proper place in Greek mythology.

Greek Totemism

In C. and M. (p. 106) I describe the social aspects of totemism. I ask if there are traces of it in Greece. Suppose, for argument's sake, that in prehistoric Greece the mouse had been a totem, as it is among the Oraons of Bengal.[78] In that case (1) places might be named from a mouse tribe; (2) mice might be held sacred per se; (3) the mouse name might be given locally to a god who superseded the mouse in pride of place; (4) images of the mouse might be associated with that of the god, (5) and used as a local badge or mark; (6) myths might be invented to explain the forgotten cause of this prominence of the mouse. If all these notes occur, they would raise a presumption in favour of totemism in the past of Greece. I then give evidence in detail, proving that all these six facts do occur among Greeks of the Troads and sporadically elsewhere. I add that, granting for the sake of argument that these traces may point to totemism in the remote past, the mouse, though originally a totem, 'need not have been an Aryan totem' (p. 116).

I offer a list of other animals closely connected with Apollo, giving him a beast's name (wolf, ram, dolphin), and associated with him in myth and art. In M. R. R. I apply similar arguments in the case of Artemis and the Bear, of Dionysus and the Bull, Demeter and the Pig, and so forth. Moreover, I account for the myths of descent of Greek human families from gods disguised as dogs, ants, serpents, bulls, and swans, on the hypothesis that kindreds who

[77] Anth. Rel. p. 122.
[78] Dalton.

originally, in totemistic fashion, traced to beasts sans phrase, later explained their own myth to themselves by saying that the paternal beast was only a god in disguise and en bonne fortune.

This hypothesis at least 'colligates the facts,' and brings them into intelligible relationship with widely-diffused savage institutions and myths.

The Greek Mouse-totem?

My theory connecting Apollo Smintheus and the place-names derived from mice with a possible prehistoric mouse-totem gave me, I confess, considerable satisfaction. But in Mr. Frazer's Golden Bough (ii. 129-132) is published a group of cases in which mice and other vermin are worshipped for prudential reasons—to get them to go away. In the Classical Review (vol. vi. 1892) Mr. Ward Fowler quotes Aristotle and Ælian on plagues of mice, like the recent invasion of voles on the Border sheep-farms. He adopts the theory that the sacred mice were adored by way of propitiating them. Thus Apollo may be connected with mice, not as a god who superseded a mouse-totem, but as an expeller of mice, like the worm-killing Heracles, and the Locust-Heracles, and the Locust-Apollo.[79] The locust is still painted red, salaamed to, and set free in India, by way of propitiating his companions.[80] Thus the Mouse-Apollo (Smintheus) would be merely a god noted for his usefulness in getting rid of mice, and any worship given to mice (feeding them, placing their images on altars, their stamp on coins, naming places after them, and so on) would be mere acts of propitiation.

There would be no mouse-totem in the background. I do not feel quite convinced—the mouse being a totem, and a sacred or tabooed animal, in India and Egypt.[81] But I am content to remain in a balance of opinion. That the Mouse is the Night (Gubernatis), or the Lightning (Grohmann), I am disinclined to believe. Philologists are very apt to jump at contending meteorological explanations of mice and such small deer without real necessity, and an anthropologist is very apt to jump at an equally unnecessary and perhaps equally undemonstrated totem.

Philological Theory

Philological mythologists prefer to believe that the forgotten

---

[79] Strabo, xiii. 613. Pausanias, i. 24, 8.
[80] Crooke, Introduction to Popular Religion of North India, p. 380.
[81] C. and M. p. 115.

meaning of words produced the results; that the wolf-born Apollo (Λυκηγενης) originally meant 'Light-born Apollo,'[82] and that the wolf came in from a confusion between λυκη, 'Light,' and λυκος, a wolf. I make no doubt that philologists can explain Sminthian Apollo, the Dog-Apollo, and all the rest in the same way, and account for all the other peculiarities of place-names, myths, works of art, local badges, and so forth. We must then, I suppose, infer that these six traits of the mouse, already enumerated, tally with the traces which actual totemism would or might leave surviving behind it, or which propitiation of mice might leave behind it, by a chance coincidence, determined by forgotten meanings of words. The Greek analogy to totemistic facts would be explained, (1) either by asking for a definition of totemism, and not listening when it is given; or (2) by maintaining that savage totemism is also a result of a world-wide malady of language, which, in a hundred tongues, produced the same confusions of thought, and consequently the same practices and institutions. Nor do I for one moment doubt that the ingenuity of philologists could prove the name of every beast and plant, in every language under heaven, to be a name for the 'inevitable dawn' (Max Müller), or for the inevitable thunder, or storm, or lightning (Kuhn-Schwartz). But as names appear to yield storm, lightning, night, or dawn with equal ease and certainty, according as the scholar prefers dawn or storm, I confess that this demonstration would leave me sceptical. It lacks scientific exactitude.

Mr. Frazer on Animals in Greek Religion

In The Golden Bough (ii. 37) Mr. Frazer, whose superior knowledge and acuteness I am pleased to confess, has a theory different from that which I (following McLennan) propounded before The Golden Bough appeared. Greece had a bull-shaped Dionysus.[83] 'There is left no room to doubt that in rending and devouring a live bull at his festival, his worshippers believed that they were killing the god, eating his flesh, and drinking his blood.'[84] Mr. Frazer concludes that there are two possible explanations of Dionysus in his bull aspect. (1) This was an expression of his character as a deity of vegetation, 'especially as the bull is a common embodiment of the corn-spirit in Northern Europe.'[85] (2) The other

---

[82] Contributions, ii. 687.
[83] Evidence in G. B. i. 325, 326.
[84] Compare Liebrecht, 'The Eaten God,' in Zur Volkskunde, p. 436.
[85] Cf. G. B. ii. 17, for evidence.

possible explanation 'appears to be the view taken by Mr. Lang, who suggests that the bull-formed Dionysus "had either been developed out of, or had succeeded to, the worship of a bull-totem."'[86]

Now, anthropologists are generally agreed, I think, that occasional sacrifices of and communion in the flesh of the totem or other sacred animals do occur among totemists.[87] But Mr. Frazer and I both admit, and indeed are eager to state publicly, that the evidence for sacrifice of the totem, and communion in eating him, is very scanty. The fact is rather inferred from rites among peoples just emerging from totemism (see the case of the Californian buzzard, in Bancroft) than derived from actual observation. On this head too much has been taken for granted by anthropologists. But I learn that direct evidence has been obtained, and is on the point of publication. The facts I may not anticipate here, but the evidence will be properly sifted, and bias of theory discounted.

To return to my theory of the development of Dionysus into a totem, or of his inheritance of the rites of a totem, Mr. Frazer says, 'Of course this is possible, but it is not yet certain that Aryans ever had totemism.'[88] Now, in writing of the mouse, I had taken care to observe that, in origin, the mouse as a totem need not have been Aryan, but adopted. People who think that the Aryans did not pass through a stage of totemism, female kin, and so forth, can always fall back (to account for apparent survivals of such things among Aryans) on 'Pre-Aryan conquered peoples,' such as the Picts. Aryans may be enticed by these bad races and become Pictis ipsis Pictiores.

Aryan Totems (?)

Generally speaking (and how delightfully characteristic of us all is this!), I see totems in Greek sacred beasts, where Mr. Frazer sees the corn-spirit embodied in a beast, and where Mr. Max Müller sees (in the case of Indra, called the bull) 'words meaning simply male, manly, strong,' an 'animal simile.'[89] Here, of course, Mr. Max Müller is wholly in the right, when a Vedic poet calls Indra 'strong bull,' or the like. Such poetic epithets do not afford the shadow of a presumption for Vedic totemism, even as a survival. Mr. Frazer agrees with me and Mr. Max Müller in this certainty. I myself say, 'If in the shape of Indra there be traces of fur and feather, they are

---

[86] M. R. R. ii. 232.
[87] G. B. ii. 90-113.
[88] In Encyclop. Brit. he thinks it 'very probable.'
[89] i. 200.

55

not very numerous nor very distinct, but we give them for what they may be worth.' I then give them.[90] To prove that I do not force the evidence, I take the Vedic text.[91] 'His mother, a cow, bore Indra, an unlicked calf.' I then give Sayana's explanation. Indra entered into the body of Dakshina, and was reborn of her. She also bore a cow. But this legend, I say, 'has rather the air of being an invention, après coup, to account for the Vedic text of calf Indra, born from a cow, than of being a genuine ancient myth.' The Vedic myth of Indra's amours in shape of a ram, I say 'will doubtless be explained away as metaphorical.' Nay, I will go further. It is perfectly conceivable to me that in certain cases a poetic epithet applied by a poet to a god (say bull, ram, or snake) might be misconceived, and might give rise to the worship of a god as a bull, or snake, or ram. Further, if civilised ideas perished, and if a race retained a bull-god, born of their degradation and confusion of mind, they might eat him in a ritual sacrifice. But that all totemistic races are totemistic, because they all first metaphorically applied animal names to gods, and then forgot what they had meant, and worshipped these animals, sans phrase, appears to me to be, if not incredible, still greatly in want of evidence.

Mr. Frazer and I

It is plain that where a people claim no connection by descent and blood from a sacred animal, are neither of his name nor kin, the essential feature of totemism is absent. I do not see that eaters of the bull Dionysus or cultivators of the pig Demeter[92] made any claim to kindred with either god. Their towns were not allied in name with pig or bull. If traces of such a belief existed, they have been sloughed off. Thus Mr. Frazer's explanation of Greek pigs and bulls and all their odd rites, as connected with the beast in which the corn-spirit is incarnate, holds its ground better than my totemistic suggestion. But I am not sure that the corn-spirit accounts for the Sminthian mouse in all his aspects, nor for the Arcadian and Attic bear-rites and myths of Artemis. Mouse and bear do appear in Mr. Frazer's catalogue of forms of the corn-spirits, taken from Mannhardt.[93] But the Arcadians, as we shall see, claimed descent from a bear, and the mouse place-names and badges of the Troad yield a hint of the same idea. The many Greek

---

[90] M. R. R. ii. 142, 148-149.
[91] R. V. iv. 18, 10.
[92] G. B. ii. 44-49.
[93] G. B. ii. 33.

family claims to descent from gods as dogs, bulls, ants, serpents, and so on, may spring from gratitude to the corn-spirit. Does Mr. Frazer think so? Nobody knows so well as he that similar claims of descent from dogs and snakes are made by many savage kindreds who have no agriculture, no corn, and, of course, no corn-spirits. These remarks, I trust, are not undiscriminating, and naturally I yield the bull Dionysus and the pig Demeter to the corn-spirit, vice totem, superseded. But I do hanker after the Arcadian bear as, at least, a possible survival of totemism. The Scottish school inspector removed a picture of Behemoth, as a fabulous animal, from the wall of a school room. But, not being sure of the natural history of the unicorn, 'he just let him bide, and gave the puir beast the benefit o' the doubt.'

Will Mr. Frazer give the Arcadian bear 'the benefit of the doubt'?

I am not at all bigoted in the opinion that the Greeks may have once been totemists. The strongest presumption in favour of the hypothesis is the many claims of descent from a god disguised as a beast. But the institution, if ever it did exist among the ancestors of the Greeks, had died out very long before Homer. We cannot expect to find traces of the prohibition to marry a woman of the same totem. In Rome we do find traces of exogamy, as among totemists. 'Formerly they did not marry women connected with them by blood.'[94] But we do not find, and would not expect to find, that the 'blood' was indicated by the common totem.

Mr. Frazer on Origin of Totemism

Mr. Frazer has introduced the term 'sex-totems,' in application to Australia. This is connected with his theory of the Origin of Totemism. I cannot quite approve of the term sex-totems.

If in Australia each sex has a protecting animal—the men a bat, the women an owl—if the slaying of a bat by a woman menaces the death of a man, if the slaying of an owl by a woman may cause the decease of a man, all that is very unlike totemism in other countries. Therefore, I ask Mr. Frazer whether, in the interests of definite terminology, he had not better give some other name than 'totem' to his Australian sex protecting animals? He might take for a local fact, a local name, and say 'Sex-kobong.'

Once more, for even we anthropologists have our bickerings, I would 'hesitate dislike' of this passage in Mr. Frazer's work:[95]

---

[94] Plutarch, Quæst. Rom. vi. McLennan, The Patriarchal Theory, p. 207, note 2.
[95] G. B. ii. 337.

'When a savage names himself after an animal, calls it his brother, and refuses to kill it, the animal is said to be his totem.' Distinguo! A savage does not name himself after his totem, any more than Mr. Frazer named himself by his clan-name, originally Norman. It was not as when Miss Betty Amory named herself 'Blanche,' by her own will and fantasy. A savage inherits his totem name, usually through the mother's side. The special animal which protects an individual savage (Zapotec, tona; Guatemalan, nagual; North America, Manitou, 'medicine') is not that savage's totem.[96] The nagual, tona, or manitou is selected for each particular savage, at birth or puberty, in various ways: in America, North and Central, by a dream in a fast, or after a dream. ('Post-hypnotic suggestion.') But a savage is born to his kin-totem. A man is born a wolf of the Delawares, his totem is the wolf, he cannot help himself. But after, or in, his medicine fast and sleep, he may choose a dormouse or a squirrel for his manitou (tona, nagual) or private protecting animal. These are quite separate from totems, as Mr. Max Müller also points out.

Of totems, I, for one, must always write in the sense of Mr. McLennan, who introduced totemism to science. Thus, to speak of 'sex-totems,' or to call the protecting animal of each individual a 'totem,' is, I fear, to bring in confusion, and to justify Mr. Max Müller's hard opinion that 'totemism' is ill-defined. For myself, I use the term in the strict sense which I have given, and in no other.

Mr. McLennan did not profess, as we saw, to know the origin of totems. He once made a guess in conversation with me, but he abandoned it. Professor Robertson Smith did not know the origin of totems. 'The origin of totems is as much a problem as the origin of local gods.'[97] Mr. Max Müller knows the origin: sign-boards are the origin, or one origin. But what was the origin of sign-boards? 'We carry the pictures of saints on our banners because we worship them; we don't worship them because we carry them as banners,' says De Brosses, an acute man. Did the Indians worship totems because they carved them on sign-boards (if they all did so), or did they carve them on sign-boards because they worshipped them?

Mr. Frazer's Theory

The Australian respects his 'sex-totem' because the life of his sex is bound up in its life. He speaks of it as his brother, and calls himself (as distinguished by his sex) by its name. As a man he is a

---

96 See G. B. ii. 332-334.
97 Religion of the Semites, p. 118.

bat, as a woman his wife is an owl. As a member of a given human kin he may be a kangaroo, perhaps his wife may be an emu. But Mr. Frazer derives totemism, all the world over, from the same origin as he assigns to 'sex-totems.' In these the life of each sex is bound up, therefore they are by each sex revered. Therefore totemism must have the same origin, substituting 'kin' or 'tribe' for sex. He gives examples from Australia, in which killing a man's totem killed the man.[98]

I would respectfully demur or suggest delay. Can we explain an American institution, a fairly world-wide institution, totemism, by the local peculiarities of belief in isolated Australia? If, in America, to kill a wolf was to kill Uncas or Chingachgook, I would incline to agree with Mr. Frazer. But no such evidence is adduced. Nor does it help Mr. Frazer to plead that the killing of an American's nagual or of a Zulu's Ihlozi kills that Zulu or American. For a nagual, as I have shown, is one thing and a totem is another; nor am I aware that Zulus are totemists. The argument of Mr. Frazer is based on analogy and on a special instance. That instance of the Australians is so archaic that it may show totemism in an early form. Mr. Frazer's may be a correct hypothesis, but it needs corroboration. However, Mr. Frazer concludes: 'The totem, if I am right, is simply the receptacle in which a man keeps his life.' Yet he never shows that a Choctaw does keep his life in his totem. Perhaps the Choctaw is afraid to let out so vital a secret. The less reticent Australian blurts it forth. Suppose the hypothesis correct. Men and women keep their lives in their naguals, private sacred beasts. But why, on this score, should a man be afraid to make love to a woman of the same nagual? Have Red Indian women any naguals? I never heard of them.

Since writing this I have read Miss Kingsley's Travels in West Africa. There the 'bush-souls' which she mentions (p. 459) bear analogies to totems, being inherited sacred animals, connected with the life of members of families. The evidence, though vaguely stated, favours Mr. Frazer's hypothesis, to which Miss Kingsley makes no allusion.

[98] G. B. ii. 337, 338.

THE VALIDITY OF ANTHROPOLOGICAL EVIDENCE

Anthropological Evidence

In all that we say of totemism, as, later, of fetishism, we rely on an enormous mass of evidence from geographers, historians, travellers, settlers, missionaries, explorers, traders, Civil Servants, and European officers of native police in Australia and Burmah. Our witnesses are of all ages, from Herodotus to our day, of many nations, of many creeds, of different theoretical opinions. This evidence, so world-wide, so diversified in source, so old, and so new, Mr. Max Müller impugns. But, before meeting his case, let us clear up a personal question.

'Positions one never held'

> 'It is not pleasant [writes our author] to have to defend positions which one never held, nor wishes to hold, and I am therefore all the more grateful to those who have pointed out the audacious misrepresentations of my real opinion in comparative mythology, and have rebuked the flippant tone of some of my eager critics' [i. 26, 27].

I must here confess to the belief that no gentleman or honest man ever consciously misrepresents the ideas of an opponent. If it is not too flippant an illustration, I would say that no bowler ever throws consciously and wilfully; his action, however, may unconsciously develop into a throw. There would be no pleasure in argument, cricket, or any other sport if we knowingly cheated. Thus it is always unconsciously that adversaries pervert, garble, and misrepresent each other's opinions; unconsciously, not 'audaciously.' If people would start from the major premise that misrepresentations, if such exist, are unconscious errors, much trouble would be spared.

Positions which I never held

Thus Mr. Max Müller never dreamed of 'audaciously misrepresenting' me when, in four lines, he made two statements about my opinions and my materials which are at the opposite pole from the accurate (i. 12): 'When I speak of the Vedic Rishis as primitive, I do not mean what Mr. A. Lang means when he calls his savages primitive.' But I have stated again and again that I don't call my savages 'primitive.' Thus 'contemporary savages may be degraded, they certainly are not primitive.'[99] 'One thing about the past of [contemporary] savages we do know: it must have been a long past.'[100] 'We do not wish to call savages primitive.'[101] All this was written in reply to the very proper caution of Dr. Fairbairn that 'savages are not primitive.' Of course they are not; that is of the essence of my theory. I regret the use of the word 'primitive' even in Primitive Culture. Savages, as a rule, are earlier, more backward than civilised races, as, of course, Mr. Max Müller admits, where language is concerned.[102] Now, after devoting several pages to showing in detail how very far from primitive even the Australian tribes are, might I (if I were ill-natured) not say that Mr. Max Müller 'audaciously misrepresents' me when he avers that I 'call my savages primitive'? But he never dreamed of misrepresenting me; he only happened not to understand my position. However, as he complains in his own case, 'it is not pleasant to have to defend positions which one never held' (i. 26), and, indeed, I shall defend no such position.

My adversary next says that my 'savages are of the nineteenth century.' It is of the essence of my theory that my savages are of many different centuries. Those described by Herodotus, Strabo, Dio Cassius, Christoval de Moluna, Sahagun, Cieza de Leon, Brébeuf, Garoilasso de la Vega, Lafitau, Nicholas Damascenus, Leo Africanus, and a hundred others, are not of the nineteenth century. This fact is essential, because the evidence of old writers, from Herodotus to Egede, corroborates the evidence of travellers, Indian Civil Servants, and missionaries of today, by what Dr. Tylor, when defending our materials, calls 'the test of recurrence.' Professor Millar used the same argument in his Origin of Rank, in the last century. Thus Mr. Max Müller unconsciously misrepresents me (and my savages) when he says that my 'savages are of the nineteenth century.' The fact is the reverse. They are of many centuries. These two unconscious misrepresentations occur in four consecutive lines.

Anthropological Evidence

In connection with this topic (the nature of anthropological

---

[99] Custom and Myth, p. 235.
[100] M. R. R. ii. 327.
[101] Op. cit. ii. 329.
[102] Lectures on Science of Language, Second Series, p. 41.

evidence), Mr. Max Müller (i. 205-207) repeats what he has often said before. Thus he cites Dr. Codrington's remarks, most valuable remarks, on the difficulty of reporting correctly about the ideas and ways of savages. I had cited the same judicious writer to the same effect,[103] and had compiled a number of instances in which the errors of travellers were exposed, and their habitual fallacies were detected. Fifteen closely printed pages were devoted by me to a criterion of evidence, and a reply to Mr. Max Müller's oft-repeated objections.

> 'When [I said] we find Dr. Codrington taking the same precautions in Melanesia as Mr. Sproat took among the Ahts, and when his account of Melanesian myths reads like a close copy of Mr. Sproat's account of Aht legends, and when both are corroborated [as to the existence of analogous savage myths] by the collections of Bleek, and Hahn, and Gill, and Castren, and Rink, in far different corners of the world; while the modern testimony of these scholarly men is in harmony with that of the old Jesuit missionaries, and of untaught adventurers who have lived for many years with savages, surely it will be admitted that the difficulty of ascertaining savage opinion has been, to a great extent, overcome.'

I also cited at length Dr. Tylor's masterly argument to the same effect, an argument offered by him to 'a great historian,' apparently.

Mr. Max Müller's Method of Controversy

Now no member of the reading public, perusing Mr. Max Müller on anthropological evidence (i. 24-26, 205-207), could guess that his cautions about evidence are not absolutely new to us. He could not guess that Dr. Tylor replied to them 'before they were made' by our present critic (I think), and that I did the same with great elaboration. Our defence of our evidence is not noticed by Mr. Max Müller. He merely repeats what he has often said before on the subject, exactly as if anthropologists were ignorant of it, and had not carefully studied, assimilated, profited by it, and answered it. Our critic and monitor might have said, 'I have examined your test of recurrences, and what else you have to urge, and, for such and such reasons, I must reject it.' Then we could reconsider our position in this new light. But Mr. Max Müller does not oblige us in this way.

---

[103] M. R. R. ii. 336.

Mr. Max Müller on our Evidence

In an earlier work, The Gifford Lectures for 1891,[104] our author had devoted more space to a criticism of our evidence. To this, then, we turn (pp. 169-180, 413-436). Passing Mr. Max Müller's own difficulties in understanding a Mohawk (which the Mohawk no doubt also felt in understanding Mr. Max Müller), we reach (p. 172) the fables about godless savages. These, it is admitted, are exploded among scholars in anthropology. So we do, at least, examine evidence. Mr. Max Müller now fixes on a flagrant case, some fables about the godless Mincopies of the Andaman Islands. But he relies on the evidence of Mr. Man. So do I, as far as it seems beyond doubt.[105] Mr. Man is 'a careful observer, a student of language, and perfectly trustworthy.' These are the reasons for which I trust him. But when Mr. Man says that the Mincopies have a god, Puluga, who inhabits 'a stone house in the sky,' I remark, 'Here the idea of the stone house is necessarily borrowed from our stone houses at Port Blair.'[106] When Mr. Man talks of Puluga's only-begotten son, 'a sort of archangel,' medium between Puluga and the angels, I 'hesitate a doubt.' Did not this idea reach the Mincopie mind from the same quarter as the stone house, especially as Puluga's wife is 'a green shrimp or an eel'? At all events, it is right to bear in mind that, as the stone house of the Mincopie heaven is almost undeniably of European origin, the only-begotten mediating son of Puluga and the green shrimp may bear traces of Christian teaching. Caution is indicated.

Does Mr. Max Müller, so strict about evidence, boggle at the stone house, the only son, the shrimp? Not he; he never hints at the shrimp! Does he point out that one anthropologist has asked for caution in weighing what the Mincopies told Mr. Man? Very far from that, he complains that 'the old story is repeated again and again' about the godless Andamans.[107] The intelligent Glasgow audience could hardly guess that anthropologists were watchful, and knew pretty well what to believe about the Mincopies. Perhaps in Glasgow they do not read us anthropologists much.

On p. 413 our author returns to the charge. He observes (as I have also observed) the often contradictory nature of our evidence. Here I may offer an anecdote. The most celebrated of living English philosophers heard that I was at one time writing a book on the

---

[104] Anthropological Religion.
[105] M. R. R. i. 171-173.
[106] Ibid. i. 172.
[107] Anth. Rel. p. 180.

'ghostly' in history, anthropology, and society, old or new, savage or civilised. He kindly dictated a letter to me asking how I could give time and pains to any such marvels. For, he argued, the most unveracious fables were occasionally told about himself in newspapers and social gossip. If evidence cannot be trusted about a living and distinguished British subject, how can it be accepted about hallucinations?

I replied, with respect, that on this principle nothing could be investigated at all. History, justice, trade, everything would be impossible. We must weigh and criticise evidence. As my friendly adviser had written much on savage customs and creeds, he best knew that conflicting testimony, even on his own chosen theme, is not peculiar to ghost stories. In a world of conflicting testimony we live by criticising it. Thus, when Mr. Max Müller says that I call my savages 'primitive,' and when I, on the other hand, quote passages in which I explicitly decline to do so, the evidence as to my views is contradictory. Yet the truth can be discovered by careful research.

The application is obvious. We must not despair of truth! As our monitor says, 'we ought to discard all evidence that does not come to us either from a man who was able himself to converse with native races, or who was at least an eye-witness of what he relates.' Precisely, that is our method. I, for one, do not take even a ghost story at second hand, much less anything so startling as a savage rite. And we discount and allow for every bias and prejudice of our witnesses. I have made a list of these idola in M. R. R. ii. 334-344.

Mr. Max Müller now gives a list of inconsistencies in descriptions of Australian Blacks. They are not Blacks, they have a dash of copper colour! Well, I never said that they had 'the sooty tinge of the African negro.' Did anybody?

Mr. Ridley thinks that all natives are called 'Murri.' Mr. Curr says 'No.' Important. We must reserve our judgment.

Missionaries say the Blacks are 'devoid of moral ideas.' What missionaries? What anthropologist believes such nonsense? There are differences of opinion about landed property, communal or private. The difference rages among historians of civilised races. So, also, as to portable property. Mr. Curr (Mr. Max Müller's witness) agrees here with those whose works I chiefly rely on.

'Mr. McLennan has built a whole social theory on the statement' (a single statement) 'made by Sir George Grey, and contradicted by Mr. Curr.' Mr. McLennan would be, I think, rather surprised at this remark; but what would he do? Why, he would re-examine the whole question, decide by the balance of evidence, and reject, modify, or retain his theory accordingly.

All sciences have to act in this way; therefore almost all

scientific theories are fluctuating. Nothing here is peculiar to anthropology. A single word, or two or three, will prove or disprove a theory of phonetic laws. Even phonetics are disputable ground.

In defence of my late friend Mr. McLennan, I must point out that if he built a whole social theory on a single statement of Sir George Grey's, and if Mr. Curr denies the truth of the statement, Mr. Frazer has produced six or seven witnesses to the truth of that very statement in other parts of the world than Australia.[108] To this circumstance we may return.

Mr. Max Müller next produces Mr. Curr's opinions about the belief in a god and morality among Australians. 'Here he really contradicts himself.' The disputable evidence about Australian marriage laws is next shown to be disputable. That is precisely why Dr. Tylor is applying to it his unrivalled diligence in accurate examination. We await his results. Finally, the contradictory evidence as to Tasmanian religion is exposed. We have no Codrington or Bleek for Tasmania. The Tasmanians are extinct, and Science should leave the evidence as to their religion out of her accounts. We cannot cross-examine defunct Tasmanians.

From all this it follows that anthropologists must sift and winnow their evidence, like men employed in every other branch of science. And who denies it? What anthropologist of mark accepts as gospel any casual traveller's tale?

The Test of Recurrences

Even for travellers' tales we have a use, we can apply to them Dr. Tylor's 'Test of Recurrences.'

> 'If two independent visitors to different countries, say a mediæval Mahommedan in Tartary and a modern Englishman in Dahomey, or a Jesuit missionary in Brazil and a Wesley an in the Fiji Islands, agree in describing some analogous art, or rite, or myth among the people they have visited, it becomes difficult or impossible to set down such correspondence to accident or wilful fraud. A story by a bushranger in Australia may perhaps be objected to as a mistake or an invention, but did a Methodist minister in Guinea conspire with him to cheat the public by telling the same story there?'

The whole passage should be read: it was anticipated by Professor Millar in his Origin of Rank, and has been restated by

---

[108] 'Totemism,' Encyclop. Brit.

myself.[109] Thus I wrote (in 1887) 'it is to be regretted that Mr. Max Müller entirely omits to mention . . . the corroboration which is derived from the undesigned coincidence of independent testimony.'

In 1891-1892 he still entirely omits to mention, to his Glasgow audience, the strength of his opponents' case. He would serve us better if he would criticise the test of recurrences, and show us its weak points.

Bias of Theory

Yes, our critic may reply, 'but Mr. Curr thinks that there is a strong tendency in observers abroad, if they have become acquainted with a new and startling theory that has become popular at home, to see confirmations of it everywhere.' So I had explicitly stated in commenting on Dr. Tylor's test of recurrences.[110] 'Travellers and missionaries have begun to read anthropological books, and their evidence is, therefore, much more likely to be biassed now by anthropological theories than it was of old.' So Mr. McLennan, in the very earliest of all writings on totemism, said: 'As the totem has not till now got itself mixed up with speculations the observers have been unbiassed.' Mr. McLennan finally declined to admit any evidence as to the savage marriage laws collected after his own theory, and other theories born from it, had begun to bias observers of barbaric tribes.

It does not quite seem to me that Mr. Max Müller makes his audience acquainted with these precautions of anthropologists, with their sedulous sifting of evidence, and watchfulness against the theoretical bias of observers. Thus he assails the faible, not the fort of our argument, and may even seem not to be aware that we have removed the faible by careful discrimination.

What opinion must his readers, who know not Mr. McLennan's works, entertain about that acute and intrepid pioneer, a man of warm temper, I admit, a man who threw out his daringly original theory at a heat, using at first such untrustworthy materials as lay at hand, but a man whom disease could not daunt, and whom only death prevented from building a stately edifice on the soil which he was the first to explore?

Our author often returns to the weakness of the evidence of travellers and missionaries.

---

[109] M. R. R. ii. 333.
[110] Ibid. ii. 335.

Concerning Missionaries

Here is an example of a vivacité in our censor. 'With regard to ghosts and spirits among the Melanesians, our authorities, whether missionaries, traders, or writers on ethnology, are troubled by no difficulties' (i. 207). Yet on this very page Mr. Max Müller has been citing the 'difficulties' which do 'trouble' a 'missionary,' Dr. Codrington. And, for my own part, when I want information about Melanesian beliefs, it is to Dr. Codrington's work that I go.[111] The doctor, himself a missionary, ex hypothesi 'untroubled by difficulties,' has just been quoted by Mr. Max Müller, and by myself, as a witness to the difficulties which trouble himself and us. What can Mr. Max Müller possibly mean? Am I wrong? Was Dr. Codrington not a missionary? At all events, he is the authority on Melanesia, a 'high' authority (i. 206).

---

[111] M. R.. R.. i. 96, 127; ii. 22, 336.

THE PHILOLOGICAL METHOD IN ANTHROPOLOGY

Mr. Max Müller as Ethnologist

Our author is apt to remonstrate with his anthropological critics, and to assure them that he also has made studies in ethnology. 'I am not such a despairer of ethnology as some ethnologists would have me.' He refers us to the assistance which he lent in bringing out Dr. Hahn's Tsuni-Goam (1881), Mr. Gill's Myths and Songs from the South Pacific (1876), and probably other examples could be added. But my objection is, not that we should be ungrateful to Mr. Max Müller for these and other valuable services to anthropology, but that, when he has got his anthropological material, he treats it in what I think the wrong way, or approves of its being so treated.

Here, indeed, is the irreconcilable difference between two schools of mythological interpretation. Given Dr. Hahn's book, on Hottentot manners and religion: the anthropologist compares the Hottentot rites, beliefs, social habits, and general ideas with those of other races known to him, savage or civilised. A Hottentot custom, which has a meaning among Hottentots, may exist where its meaning is lost, among Greeks or other 'Aryans.' A story of a Hottentot god, quite a natural sort of tale for a Hottentot to tell, may be told about a god in Greece, where it is contrary to the Greek spirit. We infer that the Greeks perhaps inherited it from savage ancestors, or borrowed it from savages.

Names of Savage Gods

This is the method, and if we can also get a scholar to analyse the names of Hottentot gods, we are all the luckier, that is, if his processes and inferences are logical. May we not decide on the logic of scholars? But, just as Mr. Max Müller points out to us the dangers attending our evidence, we point out to him the dangers attending his method. In Dr. Hahn's book, the doctor analyses the meaning of the name Tsuni-Goam and other names, discovers their original sense, and from that sense explains the myths about Hottentot divine beings.

Here we anthropologists first ask Mr. Max Müller, before accepting Dr. Hahn's etymologies, to listen to other scholars about the perils and difficulties of the philological analysis of divine names, even in Aryan languages. I have already quoted his 'defender,' Dr. Tiele. 'The philological method is inadequate and misleading, when it is a question of (1) discovering the origin of a myth, or (2) the physical explanation of the oldest myths, or (3) of accounting for the rude and obscene element in the divine legends of civilised races.'

To the two former purposes Dr. Hahn applies the philological method in the case of Tsuni-Goam. Other scholars agree with Dr. Tiele. Mannhardt, as we said, held that Mr. Max Müller's favourite etymological 'equations,' Sarameya=Hermeias; Saranyu=Demeter-Erinnys; Kentauros=Gandharvas and others, would not stand criticism. 'The method in its practical working shows a lack of the historical sense,' said Mannhardt. Curtius—a scholar, as Mr. Max Müller declares (i. 32)—says, 'It is especially difficult to conjecture the meaning of proper names, and above all of local and mythical names.'[112] I do not see that it is easier when these names are not Greek, but Hottentot, or Algonquin!

Thus Achilles may as easily mean 'holder of the people' as 'holder of stones,' i.e. a River-god! Or does Αχ suggest aqua, Achelous the River? Leto, mother of Apollo, cannot be from λαθειν, as Mr. Max Müller holds (ii. 514, 515), to which Mr. Max Müller replies, perhaps not, as far as the phonetic rules go 'which determine the formation of appellative nouns. It, indeed, would be extraordinary if it were. . . .' The phonetic rules in Hottentot may also suggest difficulties to a South African Curtius!

Other scholars agree with Curtius—agree in thinking that the etymology of mythical names is a sandy foundation for the science of mythology.

'The difficult task of interpreting mythical names has, so far, produced few certain results,' says Otto Schrader.[113]

When Dr. Hahn applies the process in Hottentot, we urge with a friendly candour these cautions from scholars on Mr. Max Müller.

A Hottentot God

In Custom and Myth (p. 207), I examine the logic by which Dr. Hahn proves Tsuni-Goam to be 'The Red Dawn.' One of his steps is to say that few means 'sore,' or 'wounded,' and that a wound is red, so he gets his 'red' in Red Dawn. But of tsu in the sense of 'red' he gives not one example, while he does give another word for

[112] Greek Etym. Engl. transl. i. 147.
[113] Sprachvergleichung und Urgeschichte, p. 431.

'red,' or 'bloody.' This may be scholarly but it is not evidence, and this is only one of many perilous steps on ground extremely scabreux, got over by a series of logical leaps. As to our quarrel with Mr. Max Müller about his friend's treatment of ethnological materials, it is this: we do not believe in the validity of the etymological method when applied to many old divine names in Greek, still less in Hottentot.

Cause of our Scepticism

Our scepticism is confirmed by the extraordinary diversity of opinion among scholars as to what the right analysis of old divine names is. Mr. Max Müller writes (i. 18): 'I have never been able to extract from my critics the title of a single book in which my etymologies and my mythological equations had been seriously criticised by real scholars.' We might answer, 'Why tell you what you know very well?' For (i. 50) you say that while Signer Canizzaro calls some of your 'equations' 'irrefutably demonstrated,' 'other scholars declare these equations are futile and impossible.' Do these other scholars criticise your equations not 'seriously'? Or are you ignorant of the names of their works?

Another case. Our author says that 'many objections were raised' to his 'equation' of Athênê=Ahanâ='Dawn' (ii. 378, 400, &c.). Have the objections ceased? Here are a few scholars who do not, or did not, accept Athênê=Ahanâ: Welcker, Benfey, Curtius, Preller, Furtwängler, Schwartz, and now Bechtel (i. 378). Mr. Max Müller thinks that he is right, but, till scholars agree, what can we do but wait?

Phonetic Bickerings

The evidence turns on theories of phonetic laws as they worked in pre-Homeric Greece. But these laws, as they apply to common ordinary words, need not, we are told, be applied so strictly to proper names, as of gods and heroes. These are a kind of comets, and their changes cannot be calculated like the changes of vulgar words, which answer to stars (i. 298). Mr. Max Müller 'formerly agreed with Curtius that phonetic rules should be used against proper names with the same severity as against ordinary nouns and verbs.' Benfey and Welcker protested, so does Professor Victor Henry. 'It is not fair to demand from mythography the rigorous observation of phonetics' (i. 387). 'This may be called backsliding,' our author confesses, and it does seem rather a 'go-as-you-please' kind of method.

Phonetic Rules

Mr. Max Müller argues at length (and, to my ignorance, persuasively) in favour of a genial laxity in the application of phonetic rules to old proper names. Do they apply to these as strictly as to ordinary words? 'This is a question that has often been asked . . . but it has never been boldly answered' (i. 297). Mr. Max Müller cannot have forgotten that Curtius answered boldly—in the negative. 'Without such rigour all attempts at etymology are impossible. For this very reason ethnologists and mythologists should make themselves acquainted with the simple principles of comparative philology.'[114]

But it is not for us to settle such disputes of scholars. Meanwhile their evidence is derived from their private interpretations of old proper names, and they differ among themselves as to whether, in such interpretations, they should or should not be governed strictly by phonetic laws. Then what Mr. Max Müller calls 'the usual bickerings' begin among scholars (i. 416). And Mr. Max Müller connects Ouranos with Vedic Varuna, while Wackernagel prefers to derive it from ουρον, urine, and this from ουρεω=Sk. Varshayâmi, to rain (ii. 416, 417), and so it goes on for years with a glorious uncertainty. If Mr. Max Müller's equations are scientifically correct, the scholars who accept them not must all be unscientific. Or else, this is not science at all.

Basis of a Science

A science in its early stages, while the validity of its working laws in application to essential cases is still undetermined, must, of course, expect 'bickerings.' But philological mythologists are actually trying to base one science, Mythology, on the still shifting and sandy foundations of another science, Phonetics. The philologists are quarrelling about their 'equations,' and about the application of their phonetic laws to mythical proper names. On the basis of this shaking soil, they propose to build another science, Mythology! Then, pleased with the scientific exactitude of their evidence, they object to the laxity of ours.

Philology in Action—Indra

As an example of the philological method with a Vedic god, take Indra. I do not think that science is ever likely to find out the

---

[114] Gr. Etym. i. 150.

whole origins of any god. Even if his name mean 'sky,' Dyaus, Zeus, we must ask what mode of conceiving 'sky' is original. Was 'sky' thought of as a person, and, if so, as a savage or as a civilised person; as a god, sans phrase; as the inanimate visible vault of heaven; as a totem, or how? Indra, like other gods, is apt to evade our observation, in his origins. Mr. Max Müller asks, 'what should we gain if we called Indra . . . a totem?' Who does? If we derive his name from the same root as 'ind-u,' raindrop, then 'his starting-point was the rain' (i. 131). Roth preferred 'idh,' 'indh,' to kindle; and later, his taste and fancy led him to 'ir,' or 'irv,' to have power over. He is variously regarded as god of 'bright firmament,' of air, of thunderstorm personified, and so forth.[115] His name is not detected among other Aryan gods, and his birth may be after the 'Aryan Separation' (ii. 752). But surely his name, even so, might have been carried to the Greeks? This, at least, should not astonish Mr. Max Müller. One had supposed that Dyaus and Zeus were separately developed, by peoples of India and Greece, from a common, pre-separation, Aryan root. One had not imagined that the Greeks borrowed divine names from Sanskrit and from India. But this, too, might happen! (ii. 506). Mr. Max Müller asks, 'Why should not a cloud or air goddess of India, whether called Svârâ or Urvasî, have supplied the first germs from which Βοωπις ποτνια Ηρη descended?' Why not, indeed, if prehistoric Greeks were in touch with India? I do not say they were not. Why should not a Vedic or Sanskrit goddess of India supply the first germs of a Greek goddess? (ii. p. 506). Why, because 'Greek gods have never been Vedic gods, but both Greek and Vedic gods have started from the same germs' (ii. 429). Our author has answered his own question, but he seems at intervals to suppose, contrary to his own principles, as I understand them, that Greek may be 'derived from' Vedic divine names, or, at least, divine names in Sanskrit. All this is rather confusing.

Obscuring the Veda

If Indra is called 'bull,' that at first only meant 'strong' (ii. 209). Yet 'some very thoughtful scholars' see traces of totemism in Indra![116] Mr. Max Müller thinks that this theory is 'obscuring the Veda by this kind of light from the Dark Continent' (America, it seems). Indra is said to have been born from a cow, like the African

---

[115] M. R. R. ii. 142.
[116] ii. 210. Cf. Oldenberg in Deutsche Rundschau, 1895, p. 205.

Heitsi Eibib.[117] There are unholy stories about Indra and rams. But I for one, as I have said already, would never deny that these may be part of the pleasant unconscious poetry of the Vedic hymnists. Indra's legend is rich in savage obscenities; they may, or may not, be survivals from savagery. At all events one sees no reason why we should not freely compare parallel savageries, and why this should 'obscure' the Veda. Comparisons are illuminating.

[117] R. V. iv. 18, 10.

CRITICISM OF FETISHISM

Mischief of Comparisons in Comparative Mythology

Not always are comparisons illuminating, it seems. Our author writes, 'It may be said—in fact, it has been said—that there can at all events be no harm in simply placing the myths and customs of savages side by side with the myths and customs of Hindus and Greeks.' (This, in fact, is the method of the science of institutions.)

'But experience shows that this is not so' (i. 195). So we must not, should not, simply place the myths and customs of savages side by side with those of Hindus and Greeks. It is taboo.

Dr. Oldenberg

Now Dr. Oldenberg, it seems, uses such comparisons of savage and Aryan faiths. Dr. Oldenberg is (i. 209) one of several 'very thoughtful scholars' who do so, who break Mr. Max Müller's prohibition. Yet (ii. 220) 'no true scholar would accept any comparison' between savage fables and the folklore of Homer and the Vedas 'as really authoritative until fully demonstrated on both sides.' Well, it is 'fully demonstrated,' or 'a very thoughtful scholar' (like Dr. Oldenberg) would not accept it. Or it is not demonstrated, and then Dr. Oldenberg, though 'a very thoughtful,' is not 'a true scholar.'

Comparisons, when odious

Once more, Mr. Max Müller deprecates the making of comparisons between savage and Vedic myths (i. 210), and then (i. 220) he deprecates the acceptance of these very comparisons 'as really authoritative until fully demonstrated.' Now, how is the validity of the comparisons to be 'fully demonstrated' if we are forbidden to make them at all, because to do so is to 'obscure' the Veda 'by light from the Dark Continent'?

A Question of Logic

I am not writing 'quips and cranks;' I am dealing quite gravely with the author's processes of reasoning. 'No true scholar' does what 'very thoughtful scholars' do. No comparisons of savage and

74

Vedic myths should be made, but yet, 'when fully demonstrated,' 'true scholars would accept them' (i 209, 220). How can comparisons be demonstrated before they are made? And made they must not be!

'Scholars'

It would be useful if Mr. Max Müller were to define 'scholar,' 'real scholar,' 'true scholar,' 'very thoughtful scholar.' The latter may err, and have erred—like General Councils, and like Dr. Oldenberg, who finds in the Veda 'remnants of the wildest and rawest essence of religion,' totemism, and the rest (i. 210). I was wont to think that 'scholar,' as used by our learned author, meant 'philological mythologist,' as distinguished from 'not-scholar,' that is, 'anthropological mythologist.' But now 'very thoughtful scholars,' even Dr. Oldenberg, Mr. Rhys, Dr. Robertson Smith, and so on, use the anthropological method, so 'scholar' needs a fresh definition. The 'not-scholars,' the anthropologists, have, in fact, converted some very thoughtful scholars. If we could only catch the true scholar! But that we cannot do till we fully demonstrate comparisons which we may not make, for fear of first 'obscuring the Veda by this kind of light from the Dark Continent.'

Anthropology and the Mysteries

It is not my affair to defend Dr. Oldenberg, whose comparisons of Vedic with savage rites I have never read, I am sorry to say. One is only arguing that the method of making such comparisons is legitimate. Thus (i. 232) controversy, it seems, still rages among scholars as to 'the object of the Eleusinian Mysteries.' 'Does not the scholar's conscience warn us against accepting whatever in the myths and customs of the Zulus seems to suit our purpose'—of explaining features in the Eleusinia? If Zulu customs, and they alone, contained Eleusinian parallels, even the anthropologist's conscience would whisper caution. But this is not the case. North American, Australian, African, and other tribes have mysteries very closely and minutely resembling parts of the rites of the Eleusinia, Dionysia, and Thesmophoria. Thus Lobeck, a scholar, describes the Rhombos used in the Dionysiac mysteries, citing Clemens Alexandrinus.[118] Thanks to Dr. Tylor's researches I was able to show (what Lobeck knew not) that the Rhombos (Australian turndun, 'Bull-roarer') is also used in Australian,

---

[118] Aglaophamus, i. 700.

African, American, and other savage religious mysteries. Now should I have refrained from producing this well-attested matter of fact till I knew Australian, American, and African languages as well as I know Greek? 'What century will it be when there will be scholars who know the dialects of the Australian blacks as well as we know the dialects of Greece?' (i. 232) asks our author. And what in the name of Eleusis have dialects to do with the circumstance that savages, like Greeks, use Rhombi in their mysteries? There are abundant other material facts, visible palpable objects and practices, which savage mysteries have in common with the Greek mysteries.[119] If observed by deaf men, when used by dumb men, instead of by scores of Europeans who could talk the native languages, these illuminating rites of savages would still be evidence. They have been seen and described often, not by 'a casual native informant' (who, perhaps, casually invented Greek rites, and falsely attributed them to his tribesmen), but by educated Europeans.

Abstract Ideas of Savages

Mr. Max Müller defends, with perfect justice, the existence of abstract ideas among contemporary savages. It appears that somebody or other has said—'we have been told' (i. 291)—'that all this' (the Mangaian theory of the universe) 'must have come from missionaries.' The ideas are as likely to have come from Hegel as from a missionary! Therefore, 'instead of looking for idols, or for totems and fetishes, we must learn and accept what the savages themselves are able to tell us. . . . ' Yes, we must learn and accept it; so I have always urged. But if the savages tell us about totems, are they not then 'casual native informants'? If a Maori tells you, as he does, of traditional hymns containing ideas worthy of Heraclitus, is that quite trustworthy; whereas, if he tells you about his idols and taboos, that cannot possibly be worthy of attention?

Perception of the Infinite

From these extraordinary examples of abstract thought in savages, our author goes on to say that his theory of 'the perception of the Infinite' as the origin of religion was received 'with a storm of unfounded obloquy' (i. 292). I myself criticised the Hibbert Lectures, in Mind;[120] on reading the essay over, I find no obloquy

---

[119] Custom and Myth, i. 29-44. M. R. R. ii. 260-273.
[120] Custom and Myth, pp. 212-242.

and no storm. I find, however, that I deny, what our author says that I assert, the primitiveness of contemporary savages.

In that essay, which, of course, our author had no reason to read, much was said about fetishism, a topic discussed by Mr. Max Müller in his Hibbert Lectures. Fetishism is, as he says, an ill word, and has caused much confusion.

Fetishism and Anthropological Method

Throughout much of his work our author's object is to invalidate the anthropological method. That method sets side by side the customs, ideas, fables, myths, proverbs, riddles, rites, of different races. Of their languages it does not necessarily take account in this process. Nobody (as we shall see) knows the languages of all, or of most, of the races whose ideas he compares. Now the learned professor establishes the 'harm done' by our method in a given instance. He seems to think that, if a method has been misapplied, therefore the method itself is necessarily erroneous. The case stands thus: De Brosses[121] first compared 'the so-called fetishes' of the Gold Coast with Greek and Roman amulets and other material objects of old religions. But he did this, we learn, without trying to find out why a negro made a fetish of a pebble, shell, or tiger's tail, and without endeavouring to discover whether the negro's motives really were the motives of his 'postulated fetish worship' in Greece, Rome, or Palestine.

Origin of Fetishes

If so, tant pis pour monsieur le President. But how does the unscientific conduct attributed to De Brosses implicate the modern anthropologist? Do we not try to find out, and really succeed sometimes in finding out, why a savage cherishes this or that scrap as a 'fetish'? I give a string of explanations in Custom and Myth (pp. 229-230). Sometimes the so-called fetish had an accidental, which was taken to be a causal, connection with a stroke of good luck. Sometimes the thing—an odd-shaped stone, say—had a superficial resemblance to a desirable object, and so was thought likely to aid in the acquisition of such objects by 'sympathetic magic.'[122]

Other 'fetishes' are revealed in dreams, or by ghosts, or by spirits appearing in semblance of animals.[123]

---

[121] Culte des Fétiches, 1760.
[122] Codrington, Journal Anthrop. Inst., Feb. 1881.
[123] C. and M. p. 230, note.

'Telekinetic' Origin of Fetishism

As I write comes in Mélusine, viii. 7, with an essay by M. Lefébure on Les Origines du Fétichisme. He derives some fetishistic practices from what the Melanesians call Mana, which, says Mr. Max Müller, 'may often be rendered by supernatural or magic power, present in an individual, a stone, or in formulas or charms' (i. 294). How, asks Mr. Lefébure, did men come to attribute this vis vivida to persons and things? Because, in fact, he says, such an unexplored force does really exist and display itself. He then cites Mr. Crookes' observations on scientifically registered 'telekinetic' performances by Daniel Dunglas Home, he cites Despine on Madame Schmitz-Baud,[124] with examples from Dr. Tylor, P. de la Rissachère, Dr. Gibier,[125] and other authorities, good or bad. Grouping, then, his facts under the dubious title of le magnétisme, M. Lefébure finds in savage observation of such facts 'the chief cause of fetishism.'

Some of M. Lefébure's 'facts' (of objects moving untouched) were certainly frauds, like the tricks of Eusapia. But, even if all the facts recorded were frauds, such impostures, performed by savage conjurers, who certainly profess[126] to produce the phenomena, might originate, or help to originate, the respect paid to 'fetishes' and the belief in Mana. But probably Major Ellis's researches into the religion of the Tshi-speaking races throw most light on the real ideas of African fetishists. The subject is vast and complex. I am content to show that, whatever De Brosses did, we do not abandon a search for the motives of the savage fetishist. Indeed, De Brosses himself did seek and find at least one African motive, 'The conjurers (jongleurs) persuade them that little instruments in their possession are endowed with a living spirit.' So far, fetishism is spiritualism.

Civilised 'Fetishism'

De Brosses did not look among civilised fetishists for the motives which he neglected among savages (i. 196). Tant pis pour monsieur le Président. But we and our method no more stand or fall with De Brosses and his, than Mr. Max Müller's etymologies stand or fall with those in the Cratylus of Plato. If, in a civilised people, ancient or modern, we find a practice vaguely styled 'fetishistic,' we examine it in its details. While we have talismans,

---

124 Rochas, Les Forces non définies, 1888, pp. 340-357, 411, 626.
125 Revue Bleue, 1890, p. 367.
126 De Brosses, p. 16.

amulets, gamblers' fétiches, I do not think that, except among some children, we have anything nearly analogous to Gold Coast fetishism as a whole. Some one seems to have called the palladium a fetish. I don't exactly know what the palladium (called a fetish by somebody) was. The hasta fetialis has been styled a fetish—an apparent abuse of language. As to the Holy Cross qua fetish, why discuss such free-thinking credulities?

Modern anthropologists—Tylor, Frazer, and the rest—are not under the censure appropriate to the illogical.

More Mischiefs of Comparison

The 'Nemesis' (i. 196) of De Brosses' errors did not stay in her ravaging progress. Fetishism was represented as 'the very beginning of religion,' first among the negroes, then among all races. As I, for one, persistently proclaim that the beginning of religion is an inscrutable mystery, the Nemesis has somehow left me scatheless, propitiated by my piety. I said, long ago, 'the train of ideas which leads man to believe in and to treasure fetishes is one among the earliest springs of religious belief.'[127] But from even this rather guarded statement I withdraw. 'No man can watch the idea of GOD in the making or in the beginning.'[128]

Still more Nemesis

The new Nemesis is really that which I have just put far from me—namely, that 'modern savages represent everywhere the Eocene stratum of religion.' They probably represent an early stage in religion, just as, teste. Mr. Max Müller, they represent an early stage in language 'In savage languages we see what we can no longer expect to see even in the most ancient Sanskrit or Hebrew. We watch the childhood of language, with all its childish pranks.'[129]

Now, if the tongues spoken by modern savages represent the 'childhood' and 'childish pranks' of language, why should the beliefs of modern savages not represent the childhood and childish pranks of religion? I am not here averring that they do so, nor even that Mr. Max Müller is right in his remark on language. The Australian blacks have been men as long as the Prussian nobility. Their language has had time to outgrow 'childish pranks,' but apparently

---

[127] C. and M. p. 214.
[128] M. R. R. i. 327.
[129] Lectures on the Science of Language, 2nd series, p. 41.

it has not made use of its opportunities, according to our critic. Does he know why?

One need not reply to the charge that anthropologists, if they are meant, regard modern savages 'as just evolved from the earth, or the sky,' or from monkeys (i. 197). 'Savages have a far-stretching unknown history behind them.' 'The past of savages, I say, must have been a long past.'[130] So, once more, the Nemesis of De Brosses fails to touch me—and, of course, to touch more learned anthropologists.

There is yet another Nemesis—the postulate that Aryans and Semites, or rather their ancestors, must have passed through the savage state. Dr. Tylor writes:—'So far as history is to be our criterion, progression is primary and degradation secondary. Culture must be gained before it can be lost.' Now a person who has not gained what Dr. Tylor calls 'culture' (not in Mr. Arnold's sense) is a man without tools, instruments, or clothes. He is certainly, so far, like a savage; is very much lower in 'culture' than any race with which we are acquainted. As a matter of hypothesis, anyone may say that man was born 'with everything handsome about him.' He has then to account for the savage elements in Greek myth and rite.

For Us or Against Us?

We now hear that the worst and last penalty paid for De Brosses' audacious comparison of savage with civilised superstitions is the postulate that Aryan and Semitic peoples have passed through a stage of savagery. 'However different the languages, customs and myths, the colour and the skulls of these modern savages might be from those of Aryan and Semitic people, the latter must once have passed through the same stage, must once have been what the negroes of the West Coast of Africa are to-day. This postulate has not been, and, according to its very nature, cannot be proved. But the mischief done by acting on such postulates is still going on, and in several cases it has come to this—that what in historical religions, such as our own, is known to be the most modern, the very last outcome, namely, the worship of relics or a belief in amulets, has been represented as the first necessary step in the evolution of all religions' (i. 197).

I really do not know who says that the prehistoric ancestors of Aryans and Semites were once in the same stage as the 'negroes of the West Coast of Africa are to-day.' These honest fellows are well acquainted with coined money, with the use of firearms, and other

---

[130] M. R. R. ii. 327 and 329.

resources of civilisation, and have been in touch with missionaries, Miss Kingsley, traders, and tourists. The ancestors of the Aryans and Semites enjoyed no such advantages. Mr. Max Müller does not tell us who says that they did. But that the ancestors of all mankind passed through a stage in which they had to develop for themselves tools, languages, clothes, and institutions, is assuredly the belief of anthropologists. A race without tools, language, clothes, pottery, and social institutions, or with these in the shape of undeveloped speech, stone knives, and 'possum or other skins, is what we call a race of savages. Such we believe the ancestors of mankind to have been—at any rate after the Fall.

Now when Mr. Max Müller began to write his book, he accepted this postulate of anthropology (i. 15). When he reached i. 197 he abandoned and denounced this postulate.

I quote his acceptance of the postulate (i. 15):—

'Even Mr. A. Lang has to admit that we have not got much beyond Fontenelle, when he wrote in the last century:

"Why are the legends [myths] about men, beasts, and gods so wildly incredible and revolting? . . . The answer is that the earliest men were in a state of almost inconceivable ignorance and savagery, and that the Greeks inherited their myths from people in the same savage stage (en un pareil état de sauvagerie). Look at the Kaffirs and Iroquois if you want to know what the earliest men were like, and remember that the very Iroquois and Kaffirs have a long past behind them"'—that is to say, are polite and cultivated compared to the earliest men of all.

Here is an uncompromising statement by Fontenelle of the postulate that the Greeks (an Aryan people) must have passed through the same stage as modern savages—Kaffirs and Iroquois—now occupy. But (i. 15) Mr. Max Müller eagerly accepts the postulate:—

'There is not a word of Fontenelle's to which I should not gladly subscribe; there is no advice of his which I have not tried to follow in all my attempts to explain the myths of India and Greece by an occasional reference to Polynesian or African folklore.'

Well, if Mr. Max Müller 'gladly subscribes,' in p. 15, to the postulate of an original universal stage of savagery, whence civilised races inherit their incredibly repulsive myths, why, in pp. 197, 198, does he denounce that very postulate as not proven, not capable of being proved, very mischievous, and one of the evils resulting from

81

our method of comparing savage and civilised rites and beliefs? I must be permitted to complain that I do not know which is Mr. Max Müller's real opinion—that given with such hearty conviction in p. 15, or that stated with no less earnestness in pp. 197, 198. I trust that I shall not be thought to magnify a mere slip of the pen. Both passages—though, as far as I can see, self-contradictory—appear to be written with the same absence of levity. Fontenelle, I own, speaks of Greeks, not Semites, as being originally savages. But I pointed out[131] that he considered it safer to 'hedge' by making an exception of the Israelites. There is really nothing in Genesis against the contention that the naked, tool-less, mean, and frivolous Adam was a savage.

The Fallacy of 'Admits'

As the purpose of this essay is mainly logical, I may point out the existence of a fallacy not marked, I think, in handbooks of Logic. This is the fallacy of saying that an opponent 'admits' what, on the contrary, he has been the first to point out and proclaim. He is thus suggested into an attitude which is the reverse of his own. Some one—I am sorry to say that I forget who he was—showed me that Fontenelle, in De l'Origine des Fables,[132] briefly stated the anthropological theory of the origin of myths, or at least of that repulsive element in them which 'makes mythology mythological,' as Mr. Max Müller says. I was glad to have a predecessor in a past less remote than that of Eusebius of Cæsarea. 'A briefer and better system of mythology,' I wrote, 'could not be devised; but the Mr. Casaubons of this world have neglected it, and even now it is beyond their comprehension.'[133] To say this in this manner is not to 'admit that we have not got much beyond Fontenelle.' I do not want to get beyond Fontenelle. I want to go back to his 'forgotten common-sense,' and to apply his ideas with method and criticism to a range of materials which he did not possess or did not investigate.

Now, on p. 15, Mr. Max Müller had got as far as accepting Fontenelle; on pp. 197, 198 he burns, as it were, that to which he had 'gladly subscribed.'

Conclusion as to our Method

All this discussion of fetishes arose out of our author's

---

[131] M. R. R. ii. 324.
[132] Paris: Œuvres, 1758, iii. 270.
[133] M. R. R. ii. 324.

selection of the subject as an example of the viciousness of our method. He would not permit us 'simply to place side by side' savage and Greek myths and customs, because it did harm (i. 195); and the harm done was proved by the Nemesis of De Brosses. Now, first, a method may be a good method, yet may be badly applied. Secondly, I have shown that the Nemesis does not attach to all of us modern anthropologists. Thirdly, I have proved (unless I am under some misapprehension, which I vainly attempt to detect, and for which, if it exists, I apologise humbly) that Mr. Max Müller, on p. 15, accepts the doctrine which he denounces on p. 197.[134] Again, I am entirely at one with Mr. Max Müller when he says (p. 210) 'we have as yet really no scientific treatment of Shamanism.' This is a pressing need, but probably a physician alone could do the work—a physician doublé with a psychologist. See, however, the excellent pages in Dr. Tylor's Primitive Culture, and in Mr. William James's Principles of Psychology, on 'Mediumship.'

---

[134] I have no concern with his criticism of Mr. Herbert Spencer (p. 203), as I entirely disagree with that philosopher's theory. The defence of 'Animism' I leave to Dr. Tylor.

THE RIDDLE THEORY

What the Philological Theory Needs

The great desideratum of the philological method is a proof that the 'Disease of Language,' ex hypothesi the most fertile source of myths, is a vera causa. Do simple poetical phrases, descriptive of heavenly phenomena, remain current in the popular mouth after the meanings of appellatives (Bright One, Dark One, &c.) have been forgotten, so that these appellatives become proper names—Apollo, Daphne, &c.? Mr. Max Müller seems to think some proof of this process as a vera causa may be derived from 'Folk Riddles.'

The Riddle Theory

We now come, therefore, to the author's treatment of popular riddles (devinettes), so common among savages and peasants. Their construction is simple: anything in Nature you please is described by a poetical periphrasis, and you are asked what it is. Thus Geistiblindr asks,

> What is the Dark One
> That goes over the earth,
> Swallows water and wood,
> But is afraid of the wind? &c.

Or we find,

> What is the gold spun from one window to another?

The answers, the obvious answers, are (1) 'mist' and (2) 'sunshine.'

In Mr. Max Müller's opinion these riddles 'could not but lead to what we call popular myths or legends.' Very probably; but this does not aid us to accept the philological method. The very essence of that method is the presumed absolute loss of the meaning of, e.g. 'the Dark One.' Before there can be a myth, ex hypothesi the words Dark One must have become hopelessly unintelligible, must have become a proper name. Thus suppose, for argument's sake only, that Cronos once meant Dark One, and was understood in that sense. People (as in the Norse riddle just cited) said, 'Cronos [i.e. the Dark One—meaning mist] swallows water and wood.' Then they forgot that Cronos was their old word for the Dark One, and was

84

mist; but they kept up, and understood, all the rest of the phrase about what mist does. The expression now ran, 'Cronos [whatever that may be] swallows water and wood.' But water comes from mist, and water nourishes wood, therefore 'Cronos swallows his children.' Such would be the development of a myth on Mr. Max Müller's system. He would interpret 'Cronos swallows his children,' by finding, if he could, the original meaning of Cronos. Let us say that he did discover it to mean 'the Dark One.' Then he might think Cronos meant 'night;' 'mist' he would hardly guess.

That is all very clear, but the point is this—in devinettes, or riddles, the meaning of 'the Dark One' is not lost:—

> 'Thy riddle is easy
> Blind Gest,
> To read'—

Heidrick answers.

What the philological method of mythology needs is to prove that such poetical statements about natural phenomena as the devinettes contain survived in the popular mouth, and were perfectly intelligible except just the one mot d'énigme—say, 'the Dark One.' That (call it Cronos='Dark One'), and that alone, became unintelligible in the changes of language, and so had to be accepted as a proper name, Cronos—a god who swallows things at large.

Where is the proof of such endurance of intelligible phrases with just the one central necessary word obsolete and changed into a mysterious proper name? The world is full of proper names which have lost their meaning—Athene, Achilles, Artemis, and so on but we need proof that poetical sayings, or riddles, survive and are intelligible except one word, which, being unintelligible, becomes a proper name. Riddles, of course, prove nothing of this kind:—

> Thy riddle is easy
> Blind Gest
> To read!

Yet Mr. Max Müller offers the suggestion that the obscurity of many of these names of mythical gods and heroes 'may be due . . . to the riddles to which they had given rise, and which would have ceased to be riddles if the names had been clear and intelligible, like those of Helios and Selene' (i. 92). People, he thinks, in making riddles 'would avoid the ordinary appellatives, and the use of little-known names in most mythologies would thus find an intelligible explanation.' Again, 'we can see how essential it was that in such mythological riddles the principal agents should not be called by

85

their regular names.' This last remark, indeed, is obvious. To return to the Norse riddle of the Dark One that swallows wood and water. It would never do in a riddle to call the Dark One by his ordinary name, 'Mist.' You would not amuse a rural audience by asking 'What is the mist that swallows wood and water?' That would be even easier than Mr. Burnand's riddle for very hot weather:—

My first is a boot, my second is a jack.

Conceivably Mr. Max Müller may mean that in riddles an almost obsolete word was used to designate the object. Perhaps, instead of 'the Dark One,' a peasant would say, 'What is the Rooky One?' But as soon as nobody knew what 'the Rooky One' meant, the riddle would cease to exist—Rooky One and all. You cannot imagine several generations asking each other—

What is the Rooky One that swallows?

if nobody knew the answer. A man who kept boring people with a mere 'sell' would be scouted; and with the death of the answerless riddle the difficult word 'Rooky' would die. But Mr. Max Müller says, 'Riddles would cease to be riddles if the names had been clear and intelligible.' The reverse is the fact. In the riddles he gives there are seldom any 'names;' but the epithets and descriptions are as clear as words can be:—

Who are the mother and children in a house, all having bald heads?—The moon and stars.

Language cannot be clearer. Yet the riddle has not 'ceased to be a riddle,' as Mr. Max Müller thinks it must do, though the words arc 'clear and intelligible.' On the other hand, if the language is not clear and intelligible, the riddle would cease to exist. It would not amuse if nobody understood it. You might as well try to make yourself socially acceptable by putting conundrums in Etruscan as by asking riddles in words not clear and intelligible in themselves, though obscure in their reference. The difficulty of a riddle consists, not in the obscurity of words or names, but in the description of familiar things by terms, clear as terms, denoting their appearance and action. The mist is described as 'dark,' 'swallowing,' 'one that fears the wind,' and so forth. The words are pellucid.

Thus 'ordinary appellatives' (i. 99) are not 'avoided' in riddles, though names (sun, mist) cannot be used in the question because they give the answer to the riddle.

For all these reasons ancient riddles cannot explain the obscurity of mythological names. As soon as the name was too obscure, the riddle and the name would be forgotten, would die together. So we know as little as ever of the purely hypothetical process by which a riddle, or popular poetical saying, remains intelligible in a language, while the mot d'énigme, becoming unintelligible, turns into a proper name—say, Cronos. Yet the belief in this process as a vera causa is essential to our author's method.

Here Mr. Max Müller warns us that his riddle theory is not meant to explain 'the obscurities of all mythological names. This is a stratagem that should be stopped from the very first.' It were more graceful to have said 'a misapprehension.'

Another 'stratagem' I myself must guard against. I do not say that no unintelligible strings of obsolete words may continue to live in the popular mouth. Old hymns, ritual speeches, and charms may and do survive, though unintelligible. They are reckoned all the more potent, because all the more mysterious. But an unintelligible riddle or poetical saying does not survive, so we cannot thus account for mythology as a disease of language.

Mordvinian Mythology

Still in the very natural and laudable pursuit of facts which will support the hypothesis of a disease of language, Mr. Max Müller turns to Mordvinian mythology. 'We have the accounts of real scholars' about Mordvinian prayers, charms, and proverbs (i. 235). The Mordvinians, Ugrian tribes, have the usual departmental Nature-gods—as Chkaï, god of the sun (chi=sun). He 'lives in the sun, or is the sun' (i. 236). His wife is the Earth or earth goddess, Védiava. They have a large family, given to incest. The morals of the Mordvinian gods are as lax as those of Mordvinian mortals. (Compare the myths and morals of Samos, and the Samian Hera.) Athwart the decent god Chkaï comes the evil god Chaitan— obviously Shaitan, a Mahommedan contamination. There are plenty of minor gods, and spirits good and bad. Dawn was a Mordvinian girl; in Australia she was a lubra addicted to lubricity.

How does this help philological mythology?

Mr. Max Müller is pleased to find solar and other elemental gods among the Mordvinians. But the discovery in no way aids his special theory. Nobody has ever denied that gods who are the sun or live in the sun are familiar, and are the centres of myths among most races. I give examples in C. and M. (pp. 104, 133, New Zealand and North America) and in M. R. R. (i. 124-135, America, Africa, Australia, Aztec, Hervey Islands, Samoa, and so on). Such Nature-myths—of sun, sky, earth—are perhaps universal; but they do not arise from disease of language. These myths deal with natural phenomena plainly and explicitly. The same is the case among the Mordvinians. 'The few names preserved to us are clearly the names of the agents behind the salient phenomena of Nature, in some cases quite intelligible, in others easily restored to their original meaning.' The meanings of the names not being forgotten, but obvious, there is no disease of language. All this does not illustrate the case of Greek divine names by resemblance, but by difference. Real scholars know what Mordvinian divine names mean. They do not know what many Greek divine names mean—as Hera, Artemis, Apollo, Athene; there is even much dispute about Demeter.

No anthropologist, I hope, is denying that Nature-myths and Nature-gods exist. We are only fighting against the philological effort to get at the elemental phenomena which may be behind Hera, Artemis, Athene, Apollo, by means of contending etymological conjectures. We only oppose the philological attempt to account for all the features in a god's myth as manifestations of the elemental qualities denoted by a name which may mean at pleasure dawn, storm, clear air, thunder, wind, twilight, water, or what you will. Granting Chkaï to be the sun, does that explain why he punishes people who bake bread on Friday? (237.) Our opponent does not seem to understand the portée of our objections. The same remarks apply to the statement of Finnish mythology here given, and familiar in the Kalewala. Departmental divine beings of natural phenomena we find everywhere, or nearly everywhere, in company, of course, with other elements of belief—totemism, worship of spirits, perhaps with monotheism in the background. That is as much our opinion as Mr. Max Müller's. What we are opposing is the theory of disease of language, and the attempt to explain, by philological conjectures, gods and heroes whose obscure names are the only sources of information.

Helios is the sun-god; he is, or lives in, the sun. Apollo may have been the sun-god too, but we still distrust the attempts to prove this by contending guesses at the origin of his name. Moreover, if all Greek gods could be certainly explained, by undisputed etymologies, as originally elemental, we still object to such logic as that which turns Saranyu into 'grey dawn.' We still object to the competing interpretations by which almost every detail of very composite myths is explained as a poetical description of some elemental process or phenomenon. Apollo may once have been the sun, but why did he make love as a dog?

Lettish Mythology

These remarks apply equally well to our author's dissertation on Lettish mythology (ii. 430 et seq.). The meaning of statements about the sun and sky 'is not to be mistaken in the mythology of the Letts.' So here is no disease of language. The meaning is not to be mistaken. Sun and moon and so on are spoken of by their natural unmistakable names, or in equally unmistakable poetical periphrases, as in riddles. The daughter of the sun hung a red cloak on a great oak-tree. This 'can hardly have been meant for anything but the red of the evening or the setting sun, sometimes called her red cloak' (ii. 439). Exactly so, and the Australians of Encounter Bay also think that the sun is a woman. 'She has a lover among the dead, who has given her a red kangaroo skin, and in this she appears at her rising.'[135] This tale was told to Mr. Meyer in 1846, before Mr. Max Müller's Dawn had become 'inevitable,' as he says.

The Lettish and Australian myths are folk-poetry; they have nothing to do with a disease of language or forgotten meanings of words which become proper names. All this is surely distinct. We proclaim the abundance of poetical Nature-myths; we 'disable' the hypothesis that they arise from a disease of language.

The Chances of Fancy

One remark has to be added. Mannhardt regarded many or most of the philological solutions of gods into dawn or sun, or thunder or cloud, as empty jeux d'esprit. And justly, for there is no name named among men which a philologist cannot easily prove to be a synonym or metaphorical term for wind or weather, dawn or sun. Whatever attribute any word connotes, it can be shown to connote some attribute of dawn or sun. Here parody comes in, and gives a not overstrained copy of the method, applying it to Mr. Gladstone, Dr. Nansen, or whom you please. And though a jest is not a refutation, a parody may plainly show the absolutely capricious character of the philological method.

---

[135] Meyer, 1846, apud Brough Smyth, Aborigines of Victoria, i. 432.

ARTEMIS

I do not here examine our author's constructive work. I have often criticised its logical method before, and need not repeat myself. The etymologies, of course, I leave to be discussed by scholars. As we have seen, they are at odds on the subject of phonetic laws and their application to mythological names. On the mosses and bogs of this Debatable Land some of them propose to erect the science of comparative mythology. Meanwhile we look on, waiting till the mosses shall support a ponderous edifice.

Our author's treatment of Artemis, however, has for me a peculiar interest (ii. 733-743). I really think that it is not mere vanity which makes me suppose that in this instance I am at least one of the authors whom Mr. Max Müller is writing about without name or reference. If so, he here sharply distinguishes between me on the one hand and 'classical scholars' on the other, a point to which we shall return. He says—I cite textually (ii. 732):—

Artemis

'The last of the great Greek goddesses whom we have to consider is Artemis. Her name, we shall see, has received many interpretations, but none that can be considered as well established—none that, even if it were so, would help us much in disentangling the many myths told about her. Easy to understand as her character seems when we confine our attention to Homer, it becomes extremely complicated when we take into account the numerous local forms of worship of which she was the object.

'We have here a good opportunity of comparing the interpretations put forward by those who think that a study of the myths and customs of uncivilised tribes can help us towards an understanding of Greek deities, and the views advocated by classical scholars[136] who draw their information, first of all, from Greek sources, and afterwards only from a comparison of the myths and customs of cognate races, more particularly from what is preserved to us in ancient Vedic literature, before they plunge into the whirlpool of ill-defined and unintelligible Kafir folklore. The former undertake to explain Artemis by showing us the progress of human intelligence from the coarsest spontaneous and primitive ideas to the most beautiful and brilliant conception of poets and sculptors.

---

[136] My italics.

They point out traces of hideous cruelties amounting almost to cannibalism, and of a savage cult of beasts in the earlier history of the goddess, who was celebrated by dances of young girls disguised as bears or imitating the movements of bears, &c. She was represented as πολυμαστος, and this idea, we are told, was borrowed from the East, which is a large term. We are told that her most ancient history is to be studied in Arkadia, where we can see the goddess still closely connected with the worship of animals, a characteristic feature of the lowest stage of religious worship among the lowest races of mankind. We are then told the old story of Lykâon, the King of Arkadia, who had a beautiful daughter called Kallisto. As Zeus fell in love with her, Hêra from jealousy changed her into a bear, and Artemis killed her with one of her arrows. Her child, however, was saved by Hermes, at the command of Zeus; and while Kallisto was changed to the constellation of the Ursa, her son Arkas became the ancestor of the Arkadians. Here, we are told, we have a clear instance of men being the descendants of animals, and of women being changed into wild beasts and stars—beliefs well known among the Cahrocs and the Kamilarois.'

* * * * *

Here I recognise Mr. Max Müller's version of my remarks on Artemis.[137] Our author has just remarked in a footnote that Schwartz 'does not mention the title of the book where his evidence has been given.' It is an inconvenient practice, but with Mr. Max Müller this reticence is by no means unusual. He 'does not mention the book where 'my 'evidence is given.'

Anthropologists are here (unless I am mistaken) contrasted with 'classical scholars who draw their information, first of all, from Greek sources.' I need not assure anyone who has looked into my imperfect works that I also drew my information about Artemis 'first of all from Greek sources,' in the original. Many of these sources, to the best of my knowledge, are not translated: one, Homer, I have translated myself, with Professor Butcher and Messrs. Leaf and Myers, my old friends.

The idea and representation of Artemis as πολυμαστος (many-breasted), 'we are told, was borrowed from the East, a large term.' I say 'she is even blended in ritual with a monstrous many-breasted divinity of Oriental religion.'[138] Is this 'large term' too vague? Then consider the Artemis of Ephesus and 'the alabaster statuette of the goddess' in Roscher's Lexikon, p. 558. Compare, for

[137] M. R. R. ii. 208-221.
[138] Ibid. ii. 209.

91

an Occidental parallel, the many-breasted goddess of the maguey plant, in Mexico.[139] Our author writes, 'we are told that Artemis's most ancient history is to be studied in Arkadia.' My words are, 'The Attic and Arcadian legends of Artemis are confessedly among the oldest.' Why should 'Attic' and the qualifying phrase be omitted?

Otfried Müller

Mr. Max Müller goes on—citing, as I also do, Otfried Müller:— 'Otfried Müller in 1825 treated the same myth without availing himself of the light now to be derived from the Cahrocs and the Kamilarois. He quoted Pausanias as stating that the tumulus of Kallisto was near the sanctuary of Artemis Kallistê, and he simply took Kallisto for an epithet of Artemis, which, as in many other cases, had been taken for a separate personality.' Otfried also pointed out, as we both say, that at Brauron, in Attica, Artemis was served by young maidens called αρκτοι (bears); and he concluded, 'This cannot possibly be a freak of chance, but the metamorphosis [of Kallisto] has its foundation in the fact that the animal [the bear] was sacred to the goddess.'

Thus it is acknowledged that Artemis, under her name of Callisto, was changed into a she-bear, and had issue, Arkas—whence the Arcadians. Mr. Max Müller proceeds (ii. 734)—'He [Otfried] did not go so far as some modern mythologists who want us to believe that originally the animal, the she-bear, was the goddess, and that a later worship had replaced the ancient worship of the animal pur et simple.'

Did I, then, tell anybody that 'originally the she-bear was the goddess'? No, I gave my reader, not a dogma, but the choice between two alternative hypotheses. I said, 'It will become probable that the she-bear actually was the goddess at an extremely remote period, or at all events that the goddess succeeded to, and threw her protection over, an ancient worship of the animal' (ii. 212, 213).

Mr. Max Müller's error, it will be observed, consists in writing 'and' where I wrote 'or.' To make such rather essential mistakes is human; to give references is convenient, and not unscholarly.

In fact, this is Mr. Max Müller's own opinion, for he next reports his anonymous author (myself) as saying ('we are now told'), 'though without any reference to Pausanias or any other Greek writers, that the young maidens, the αρκτοι, when dancing around Artemis, were clad in bearskins, and that this is a pretty

---

[139] M. R. R. ii. 218.

frequent custom in the dances of totemic races. In support of this, however, we are not referred to really totemic races . . . but to the Hirpi of Italy, and to the Διος κωδων in Egypt.' Of course I never said that the αρκτοι danced around Artemis! I did say, after observing that they were described as 'playing the bear,' 'they even in archaic ages wore bear-skins,' for which I cited Claus[140] and referred to Suchier,[141] including the reference in brackets to indicate that I borrowed it from a book which I was unable to procure.[142] I then gave references for the classical use of a saffron vest by the αρκτοι.

Beast Dances

For the use of beast-skins in such dances among totemists I cite Bancroft (iii. 168) and (M. R. R. ii. 107) Robinson[143] (same authority). I may now also refer to Robertson Smith:[144] 'the meaning of such a disguise [a fish-skin, among the Assyrians] is well known from many savage rituals; it means that the worshipper presents himself as a fish,' as a bear, or what not.[145] Doubtless I might have referred more copiously to savage rituals, but really I thought that savage dances in beast-skins were familiar from Catlin's engravings of Mandan and Nootka wolf or buffalo dances. I add that the Brauronian rites 'point to a time when the goddess was herself a bear,' having suggested an alternative theory, and added confirmation.[146] But I here confess that while beast-dances and wearing of skins of sacred beasts are common, to prove these sacred beasts to be totems is another matter. It is so far inferred rather than demonstrated. Next I said that the evolution of the bear into the classical Artemis 'almost escapes our inquiry. We find nothing more akin to it than the relation borne by the Samoan gods to the various totems in which they are supposed to be manifest.' This Mr. Max Müller quotes (of course, without reference or marks of quotation) and adds, 'pace Dr. Codrington.' Have I incurred Dr. Codrington's feud? He doubts or denies totems in Melanesia. Is

---

[140] De Dianæ Antiquissima apud Græcos Natura, p. 76. Vratislaw, 1881.

[141] De Diane Brauron, p. 33. Compare, for all the learning, Mr. Farnell, in Cults of the Greek States.

[142] M. R. R. i. x.

[143] Life in California, pp. 241, 303.

[144] Religion of the Semites, p. 274.

[145] See also Mr. Frazer, Golden Bough, ii. 90-94; and Robertson Smith, op. cit. pp. 416-418.

[146] Apostolius, viii. 19; vii. 10.

Samoa in Melanesia, par exemple?[147] Our author (i. 206) says that 'Dr. Codrington will have no totems in his islands.' But Samoa is not one of the doctor's fortunate isles. For Samoa I refer, not to Dr. Codrington, but to Mr. Turner.[148] In Samoa the 'clans' revere each its own sacred animals, 'but combine with it the belief that the spiritual deity reveals itself in each separate animal.'[149] I expressly contrast the Samoan creed with 'pure totemism.'[150]

So much for our author's success in stating and criticising my ideas. If he pleases, I will not speak of Samoan totems, but of Samoan sacred animals. It is better and more exact.

The View of Classical Scholars

They (ii. 735) begin by pointing out Artemis's connection with Apollo and the moon. So do I! 'If Apollo soon disengages himself from the sun . . . Artemis retains as few traces of any connection with the moon.'[151] 'If Apollo was of solar origin,' asks the author (ii. 735), 'what could his sister Artemis have been, from the very beginning, if not some goddess connected with the moon?' Very likely; quis negavit? Then our author, like myself (loc. cit.), dilates on Artemis as 'sister of Apollo.' 'Her chapels,' I say, 'are in the wild wood; she is the abbess of the forest nymphs,' 'chaste and fair, the maiden of the precise life.' How odd! The classical scholar and I both say the same things; and I add a sonnet to Artemis in this aspect, rendered by me from the Hippolytus of Euripides. Could a classical scholar do more? Our author then says that the Greek sportsman 'surprised the beasts in their lairs' by night. Not very sportsmanlike! I don't find it in Homer or in Xenophon. Oh for exact references! The moon, the nocturnal sportswoman, is Artemis: here we have also the authority of Théodore de Banville (Diane court dans la noire forêt). And the nocturnal hunt is Dian's; so she is protectress of the chase. Exactly what I said![152]

All this being granted by me beforehand (though possibly that might not be guessed from my critic), our author will explain Artemis's human sacrifice of a girl in a fawn-skin—bloodshed, bear and all—with no aid from Kamilarois, Cahrocs, and Samoans.

---

[147] Melanesians, p. 32.
[148] Samoa, p. 17.
[149] M. R. R. ii. 33.
[150] See also Frazer, Golden Bough, ii. 92.
[151] M. R. R. ii. 208.
[152] M. R. R. ii. 209.

Mr. Max Müller's Explanation

Greek races traced to Zeus—usually disguised, for amorous purposes, as a brute. The Arcadians had an eponymous heroic ancestor, 'Areas;' they also worshipped Artemis. Artemis, as a virgin, could not become a mother of Areas by Zeus, or by anybody. Callisto was also Artemis. Callisto was the mother of Areas. But, to save the character of Artemis, Callisto was now represented as one of her nymphs. Then, Areas reminding the Arcadians of αρκτος (a bear), while they knew the Bear constellation, 'what was more natural than that Callisto should be changed into an arktos, a she-bear . . . placed by Zeus, her lover, in the sky' as the Bear?

Nothing could be more natural to a savage; they all do it.[153] But that an Aryan, a Greek, should talk such nonsense as to say that he was the descendant of a bear who was changed into a star, and all merely because 'Areas reminded the Arcadians of arktos,' seems to me an extreme test of belief, and a very unlikely thing to occur.

Wider Application of the Theory

Let us apply the explanation more widely. Say that a hundred animal names are represented in the known totem-kindreds of the world. Then had each such kin originally an eponymous hero whose name, like that of Areas in Arcady, accidentally 'reminded' his successors of a beast, so that a hundred beasts came to be claimed as ancestors? Perhaps this was what occurred; the explanation, at all events, fits the wolf of the Delawares and the other ninety-nine as well as it fits the Arcades. By a curious coincidence all the names of eponymous heroes chanced to remind people of beasts. But whence come the names of eponymous heroes? From their tribes, of course—Ion from Ionians, Dorus from Dorians, and so on. Therefore (in the hundred cases) the names of the tribes derive from names of animals. Indeed, the names of totem-kins are the names of animals—wolves, bears, cranes. Mr. Max Müller remarks that the name 'Arcades' may come from αρκτος, a bear (i. 738); so the Arcadians (Proselenoi, the oldest of races, 'men before the moon') may be—Bears. So, of course (in this case), they would necessarily be Bears before they invented Areas, an eponymous hero whose name is derived from the pre-existing tribal name. His name, then, could not, before they invented it, remind them of a bear. It was from their name Αρκτοι (Bears) that they developed his name Areas, as in all such cases of eponymous heroes. I slightly

---

[153] Custom and Myth, 'Star Myths.'

incline to hold that this is exactly what occurred. A bear-kin claimed descent from a bear, and later, developing an eponymous hero, Areas, regarded him as son of a bear. Philologically 'it is possible;' I say no more.

The Bear Dance

'The dances of the maidens called αρκτοι, would receive an easy interpretation. They were Arkades, and why not αρκτοι (bears)?' And if αρκτοι, why not clad in bear-skins, and all the rest? (ii. 738). This is our author's explanation; it is also my own conjecture. The Arcadians were bears, knew it, and possibly danced a bear dance, as Mandans or Nootkas dance a buffalo dance or a wolf dance. But all such dances are not totemistic. They have often other aims. One only names such dances totemistic when performed by people who call themselves by the name of the animal represented, and claim descent from him. Our author says genially, 'if anybody prefers to say that the arctos was something like a totem of the Arcadians . . . why not?' But, if the arctos was a totem, that fact explains the Callisto story and Attic bear dance, while the philological theory—Mr. Max Müller's theory—does not explain it. What is oddest of all, Mr. Max Müller, as we have seen, says that the bear-dancing girls were 'Arkades.' Now we hear of no bear dances in Arcadia. The dancers were Athenian girls. This, indeed, is the point. We have a bear Callisto (Artemis) in Arcady, where a folk etymology might explain it by stretching a point. But no etymology will explain bear dances to Artemis in Attica. So we find bears doubly connected with Artemis. The Athenians were not Arcadians.

As to the meaning and derivation of Artemis, or Artamis, our author knows nothing (ii. 741). I say, 'even Αρκτεμις (αρκτος, bear) has occurred to inventive men.' Possibly I invented it myself, though not addicted to etymological conjecture.

THE FIRE-WALK

The Method of Psychical Research

As a rule, mythology asks for no aid from Psychical Research. But there are problems in religious rite and custom where the services of the Cendrillon of the sciences, the despised youngest sister, may be of use. As an example I take the famous mysterious old Fire-rite of the Hirpi, or wolf-kin, of Mount Soracte. I shall first, following Mannhardt, and making use of my own trifling researches in ancient literature, describe the rite itself.

Mount Soracte

Everyone has heard of Mount Soracte, white with shining snow, the peak whose distant cold gave zest to the blazing logs on the hearth of Horace. Within sight of his windows was practised, by men calling themselves 'wolves' (Hirpi), a rite of extreme antiquity and enigmatic character. On a peak of Soracte, now Monte di Silvestre, stood the ancient temple of Soranus, a Sabine sun-god.[154] Virgil[155] identifies Soranus with Apollo. At the foot of the cliff was the precinct of Feronia, a Sabine goddess. Mr. Max Müller says that Feronia corresponds to the Vedic Bhuranyu, a name of Agni, the Vedic fire-god (ii. 800). Mannhardt prefers, of course, a derivation from far (grain), as in confarreatio, the ancient Roman bride-cake form of marriage. Feronia Mater=Sanskrit bharsani mata, Getreide Mutter.[156] It is a pity that philologists so rarely agree in their etymologies. In Greek the goddess is called Anthephorus, Philostephanus, and even Persephone—probably the Persephone of flowers and garlands.[157]

Hirpi Sorani

Once a year a fête of Soranus and Feronia was held, in the precinct of the goddess at Soracte. The ministrants were members of certain local families called Hirpi (wolves). Pliny says,[158] 'A few families, styled Hirpi, at a yearly sacrifice, walk over a burnt pile of

---

[154] L. Preller, Röm. Myth. p. 239, gives etymologies.
[155] Æn. xi. 785.
[156] A. W. F. p. 328.
[157] Dionys. Halic. iii. 32.
[158] Hist. Nat. vii. 2.

wood, yet are not scorched. On this account they have a perpetual exemption, by decree of the Senate, from military and all other services.' Virgil makes Aruns say,[159] 'Highest of gods, Apollo, guardian of Soracte, thou of whom we are the foremost worshippers, thou for whom the burning pile of pinewood is fed, while we, strong in faith, walk through the midst of the fire, and press our footsteps in the glowing mass. . . .' Strabo gives the same facts. Servius, the old commentator on Virgil, confuses the Hirpi, not unnaturally, with the Sabine 'clan,' the Hirpini. He says,[160] 'Varro, always an enemy of religious belief, writes that the Hirpini, when about to walk the fire, smear the soles of their feet with a drug' (medicamentum). Silius Italicus (v. 175) speaks of the ancient rite, when 'the holy bearer of the bow (Apollo) rejoices in the kindled pyres, and the ministrant thrice gladly bears entrails to the god through the harmless flames.' Servius gives an ætiological myth to account for the practice. 'Wolves came and carried off the entrails from the fire; shepherds, following them, were killed by mortal vapours from a cave; thence ensued a pestilence, because they had followed the wolves. An oracle bade them "play the wolf," i.e. live on plunder, whence they were called Hirpi, wolves,' an attempt to account for a wolf clan-name. There is also a story that, when the grave of Feronia seemed all on fire, and the people were about carrying off the statue, it suddenly grew green again.[161]

Mannhardt decides that the so-called wolves leaped through the sun-god's fire, in the interest of the health of the community. He elucidates this by a singular French popular custom, held on St. John's Eve, at Jumièges. The Brethren of the Green Wolf select a leader called Green Wolf, there is an ecclesiastical procession, curé and all, a souper maigre, the lighting of the usual St. John's fire, a dance round the fire, the capture of next year's Green Wolf, a mimicry of throwing him into the fire, a revel, and next day a loaf of pain bénit, above a pile of green leaves, is carried about.[162]

The wolf, thinks Mannhardt, is the Vegetation-spirit in animal form. Many examples of the 'Corn-wolf' in popular custom are given by Mr. Frazer in The Golden Bough (ii. 3-6). The Hirpi of Soracte, then, are so called because they play the part of Corn-wolves, or Korndämonen in wolf shape. But Mannhardt adds, 'this seems, at least, to be the explanation.' He then combats Kuhn's

---

[159] Æn. xi. 784.
[160] Æn. xi. 787.
[161] Serv. Æn. vii. 800.
[162] Authorities in A. F. W. K. p. 325.

theory of Feronia as lightning goddess.[163]   He next compares the strange Arcadian cannibal rites on Mount Lycæus.[164]

Mannhardt's Deficiency

In all this ingenious reasoning, Mannhardt misses a point. What the Hirpi did was not merely to leap through light embers, as in the Roman Palilia, and the parallel doings in Scotland, England, France, and elsewhere, at Midsummer (St. John's Eve). The Hirpi would not be freed from military service and all other State imposts for merely doing what any set of peasants do yearly for nothing. Nor would Varro have found it necessary to explain so easy and common a feat by the use of a drug with which the feet were smeared. Mannhardt, as Mr. Max Müller says, ventured himself little 'among red skins and black skins.' He read Dr. Tylor, and appreciated the method of illustrating ancient rites and beliefs from the living ways of living savages.[165] But, in practice, he mainly confined himself to illustrating ancient rites and beliefs by survival in modern rural folk-lore. I therefore supplement Mannhardt's evidence from European folk-lore by evidence from savage life, and by a folk-lore case which Mannhardt did not know.

The Fire-walk

A modern student is struck by the cool way in which the ancient poets, geographers, and commentators mention a startling circumstance, the Fire-walk. The only hint of explanation is the statement that the drug or juice of herbs preserved the Hirpi from harm. That theory may be kept in mind, and applied if it is found useful. Virgil's theory that the ministrants walk, pietate freti, corresponds to Mrs. Wesley's belief, when, after praying, she 'waded the flames' to rescue her children from the burning parsonage at Epworth. The hypothesis of Iamblichus, when he writes about the ecstatic or 'possessed' persons who cannot be injured by fire, is like that of modern spiritualists—the 'spirit' or 'dæmon' preserves them unharmed.

I intentionally omit cases which are vaguely analogous to that of the Hirpi. In Icelandic sagas, in the Relations of the old Jesuit missionaries, in the Travels of Pallas and Gmelin, we hear of medicine-men and Berserks who take liberties with red-hot metal,

---

[163] Herabkunft, p. 30.
[164] Pausanias, viii. 385.
[165] A. W. F. K. xxii. xxiii.

live coals, and burning wood. Thus in the Icelandic Flatey Book (vol. i. p. 425) we read about the fighting evangelist of Iceland, a story of Thangbrandr and the foreign Berserkir. 'The Berserkir said: "I can walk through the burning fire with my bare feet." Then a great fire was made, which Thangbrandr hallowed, and the Berserkir went into it without fear, and burned his feet'—the Christian spell of Thangbrandr being stronger than the heathen spell of the Berserkir. What the saga says is not evidence, and some of the other tales are merely traditional. Others may be explained, perhaps, by conjuring. The mediæval ordeal by fire may also be left on one side. In 1826 Lockhart published a translation of the Church Service for the Ordeal by Fire, a document given, he says, by Büsching in Die Vorzeit for 1817. The accused communicates before carrying the red-hot iron bar, or walking on the red-hot ploughshare. The consecrated wafer is supposed to preserve him from injury, if he be guiltless. He carries the iron for nine yards, after which his hands are sealed up in a linen cloth and examined at the end of three days. 'If he be found clear of scorch or scar, glory to God.' Lockhart calls the service 'one of the most extraordinary records of the craft, the audacity, and the weakness of mankind.'[166]

The fraud is more likely to have lain in the pretended failure to find scorch or scar than in any method of substituting cold for hot iron, or of preventing the metal from injuring the subject of the ordeal. The rite did not long satisfy the theologians and jurists of the Middle Ages. It has been discussed by Lingard in his History of England, and by Dr. E. B. Tylor in Primitive Culture.

For the purpose of the present inquiry I also omit all the rites of leaping sportfully, and of driving cattle through light fires. Of these cases, from the Roman Palilia, or Parilia, downwards, there is a useful collection in Brand's Popular Antiquities under the heading 'Midsummer Eve.' One exception must be made for a passage from Torreblanca's Demonologia (p. 106). People are said 'pyras circumire et transilire in futuri mali averruncatione'—to 'go round about and leap over lighted pyres for the purpose of averting future evils,' as in Mannhardt's theory of the Hirpi. This may be connected with the Bulgarian rite, to be described later, but, as a rule, in all these instances, the fire is a light one of straw, and no sort of immunity is claimed by the people who do not walk through, but leap across it.

These kinds of analogous examples, then, it suffices merely to mention. For the others, in all affairs of this sort, the wide diffusion of a tale of miracle is easily explained. The fancy craves for

---

[166] Janus, pp. 44-49.

miracles, and the universal mode of inventing a miracle is to deny the working, on a given occasion, of a law of Nature. Gravitation was suspended, men floated in air, inanimate bodies became agile, or fire did not burn. No less natural than the invention of the myth is the attempt to feign it by conjuring or by the use of some natural secret. But in the following modern instances the miracle of passing through the fire uninjured is apparently feigned with considerable skill, or is performed by the aid of some secret of Nature not known to modern chemistry. The evidence is decidedly good enough to prove that in Europe, India, and Polynesia the ancient rite of the Hirpi of Soracte is still a part of religious or customary ceremony.

Fijian Fire-walk

The case which originally drew my attention to this topic is that given by Mr. Basil Thomson in his South Sea Yarns (p. 195). Mr. Thomson informs me that he wrote his description on the day after he witnessed the ceremony, a precaution which left no room for illusions of memory. Of course, in describing a conjuring trick, one who is not an expert records, not what actually occurred, but what he was able to see, and the chances are that he did not see, and therefore omits, an essential circumstance, while he misstates other circumstances. I am informed by Mrs. Steel, the author of The Potter's Thumb and other stories of Indian life, that, in watching an Indian conjurer, she generally, or frequently, detects his method. She says that the conjurer often begins by whirling rapidly before the eyes of the spectators a small polished skull of a monkey, and she is inclined to think that the spectators who look at this are, in some way, more easily deluded. These facts are mentioned that I may not seem unaware of what can be said to impugn the accuracy of the descriptions of the Fire Rite, as given by Mr. Thomson and other witnesses.

Mr. Thomson says that the Wesleyan missionaries have nearly made a clean sweep of all heathen ceremonial in Fiji. 'But in one corner of Fiji, the island of Nbengga, a curious observance of mythological origin has escaped the general destruction, probably because the worthy iconoclasts had never heard of it.' The myth tells how the ancestor of the clan received the gift of fire-walking from a god, and the existence of the myth raises a presumption in favour of the antiquity of the observance.

* * * * *

'Once every year the masáwe, a dracæna that grows in profusion on the grassy hillsides of the island, becomes fit to yield

101

the sugar of which its fibrous root is full. To render it fit to eat, the roots must be baked among hot stones for four days. A great pit is dug, and filled with large stones and blazing logs, and when these have burned down, and the stones are at white heat, the oven is ready for the masáwe. It is at this stage that the clan Na Ivilankata, favoured of the gods, is called on to "leap into the oven" (rikata na lovo), and walk unharmed upon the hot stones that would scorch and wither the feet of any but the descendants of the dauntless Tui Nkualita. Twice only had Europeans been fortunate enough to see the masáwe cooked, and so marvellous had been the tales they told, and so cynical the scepticism with which they had been received, that nothing short of another performance before witnesses and the photographic camera would have satisfied the average "old hand."

'As we steamed up to the chiefs village of Waisoma, a cloud of blue smoke rolling up among the palms told us that the fire was newly lighted. We found a shallow pit, nineteen feet wide, dug in the sandy soil, a stone's throw from high-water mark, in a small clearing among the cocoanuts between the beach and the dense forest. The pit was piled high with great blazing logs and round stones the size of a man's head. Mingled with the crackling roar of the fire were loud reports as splinters flew off from the stones, warning us to guard our eyes. A number of men were dragging up more logs and rolling them into the blaze, while, above all, on the very brink of the fiery pit, stood Jonathan Dambea, directing the proceedings with an air of noble calm. As the stones would not be hot enough for four hours, there was ample time to hear the tradition that warrants the observance of the strange ceremony we were to see.

'When we were at last summoned, the fire had been burning for more than four hours. The pit was filled with a white-hot mass shooting out little tongues of white flame, and throwing out a heat beside which the scorching sun was a pleasant relief. A number of men were engaged, with long poles to which a loop of thick vine had been attached, in noosing the pieces of unburnt wood by twisting the pole, like a horse's twitch, until the loop was tight, and dragging the log out by main force. When the wood was all out there remained a conical pile of glowing stones in the middle of the pit. Ten men now drove the butts of green saplings into the base of the pile, and held the upper end while a stout vine was passed behind the row of saplings. A dozen men grasped each end of the vine, and with loud shouts hauled with all their might. The saplings, like the teeth of an enormous rake, tore through the pile of stones, flattening them out towards the opposite edge of the pit. The saplings were then driven in on the other side and the stones raked in the opposite direction, then sideways, until the bottom of the pit was covered with an even layer of hot stones. This process had taken fully half an hour, but any doubt as to the heat of the stones at the end was set at rest by the tongues of flame that played continually among them. The cameras were hard at work, and a large crowd of people pressed inwards towards the pit as the moment drew near. They were all excited except Jonathan, who preserved, even in the supreme moment, the air of holy calm that never leaves his face. All eyes are fixed expectant on the dense bush behind the clearing, whence the Shadrachs, Meshachs and Abednegos of the Pacific are to emerge. There is a cry of "Vutu! Vutu!" and forth from the bush, two and two, march fifteen men, dressed in garlands and fringes. They tramp straight to the brink of the pit. The leading pair show something like fear in their faces, but do not pause, perhaps because the rest would force them to move forward. They step down upon the stones and continue their march round the pit, planting their feet squarely and firmly on each stone. The cameras snap, the crowd surges forward, the bystanders fling in great bundles of green leaves. But the bundles strike the last man of the procession and cut him off from his fellows; so he stays where he is, trampling down the leaves as they are thrown to line the pit, in a dense cloud of steam from the boiling sap. The rest leap back to his assistance, shouting and trampling, and the pit turns into the mouth of an Inferno, filled with dusky frenzied fiends, half seen through the dense volume that rolls up to heaven and darkens the sunlight. After the leaves, palm-leaf baskets of the dracæna root are flung to them, more leaves, and then bystanders and every one join in shovelling earth over all till the pit is gone, and a smoking mound of fresh earth takes its place. This will keep hot for four days, and then the masáwe will be cooked.

'As the procession had filed up to the pit, by a preconcerted arrangement with the noble Jonathan, a large stone had been hooked out of the pit to the feet of one of the party, who poised a pocket-handkerchief over it, and dropped it lightly upon the stone when the first man leapt into the oven, and snatched what remained of it up as the last left the stones. During the fifteen or twenty seconds it lay there every fold that touched the stone was charred, and the rest of it scorched yellow. So the stones were not cool. We caught four or five of the performers as they came out, and closely examined their feet. They were cool, and showed no trace of scorching, nor were their anklets of dried tree-fern leaf burnt. This, Jonathan explained, is part of the miracle; for dried tree-fern is as combustible as tinder, and there were flames shooting out among the stones. Sceptics had affirmed that the skin of a Fijian's foot

103

being a quarter of an inch thick, he would not feel a burn. Whether this be true or not of the ball and heel, the instep is covered with skin no thicker than our own, and we saw the men plant their insteps fairly on the stone.'

* * * * *

Mr. Thomson's friend, Jonathan, said that young men had been selected because they would look better in a photograph, and, being inexperienced, they were afraid. A stranger would share the gift if he went in with one of the tribe. Some years ago a man fell and burned his shoulders. 'Any trick?' 'Here Jonathan's ample face shrunk smaller, and a shadow passed over his candid eye.' Mr. Thomson concludes: 'Perhaps the Na Ivilankata clan have no secret, and there is nothing wonderful in their performance; but, miracle or not, I am very glad I saw it.' The handkerchief dropped on the stone is 'alive to testify to it.' Mr. Thomson's photograph of the scene is ill-developed, and the fumes of steam somewhat interfere with the effect. A rough copy is published in Folk-Lore for September, 1895, but the piece could only be reproduced by a delicate drawing with the brush.

The parallel to the rite of the Hirpi is complete, except that red-hot stones, not the pyre of pine-embers, is used in Fiji. Mr. Thomson has heard of a similar ceremony in the Cook group of islands. As in ancient Italy, so in Fiji, a certain clan have the privilege of fire-walking. It is far enough from Fiji to Southern India, as it is far enough from Mount Soracte to Fiji. But in Southern India the Klings practise the rite of the Hirpi and the Na Ivilankata. I give my informant's letter exactly as it reached me, though it has been published before in Longman's Magazine:

Kling Fire-walk

'Dear Sir,—Observing from your note in Longman's Magazine that you have mislaid my notes re fire-walking, I herewith repeat them. I have more than once seen it done by the "Klings," as the low-caste Tamil-speaking Hindus from Malabar are called, in the Straits Settlements. On one occasion I was present at a "fire-walking" held in a large tapioca plantation in Province Wellesley, before many hundreds of spectators, all the Hindu coolies from the surrounding estates being mustered. A trench had been dug about twenty yards long by six feet wide and two deep. This was piled with faggots and small wood four or five feet high. This was lighted at midday, and by four p.m. the trench was a bed of red-hot ashes, the heat from which was so intense that the men who raked and levelled it with long poles could not stand it for more than a minute at a time. A few yards from the end of the trench a large hole had been dug and filled with water. When all was ready, six men, ordinary coolies, dressed only in their "dholis," or loin-cloths, stepped out of the crowd, and, amidst tremendous excitement and a horrible noise of conches and drums, passed over the burning trench from end to end, in single file, at a quick walk, plunging one after the other into the water. Not one of them showed the least sign of injury. They had undergone some course of preparation by their priest, not a Brahman, but some kind of devil-doctor or medicine-man, and, as I understood it, they took on themselves and expiated the sins of the Kling community for the past year (a big job, if thieving and lying count; probably not). They are not, however, always so lucky, for I heard that on the next occasion one of the men fell and was terribly burnt, thus destroying the whole effect of the ceremony. I do not think this to be any part of the Brahmanical religion, though the ordeal by fire as a test of guilt is, or was, in use all over India. The fact is that the races of Southern India, where the Aryan element is very small, have kept all their savage customs and devil-worship under the form of Brahmanism.

'Another curious feat I saw performed at Labuan Deli, in Sumatra, on the Chinese New Year. A Chinaman of the coolie class was squatted stark naked on the roadside, holding on his knees a brass pan the size of a wash-hand basin, piled a foot high with red-hot charcoal. The heat reached one's face at two yards, but if it had been a tray of ices the man couldn't have been more unconcerned. There was a crowd of Chinese round him, all eagerly asking questions, and a pile of coppers accumulating beside him. A Chinese shopkeeper told me that the man "told fortunes," but from the circumstance of a gambling-house being close by, I concluded that his customers were getting tips on a system.

'Hoping these notes may be of service to you,
'I remain,
'Yours truly,
'STEPHEN PONDER.'

* * * * *

In this rite the fire-pit is thrice as long (at a rough estimate) as that of the Fijians. The fire is of wooden embers, not heated stones. As in Fiji, a man who falls is burned, clearly suggesting that the feet and legs, but not the whole body, are in some way prepared to resist the fire. As we shall find to be the practice in Bulgaria, the celebrants place their feet afterwards in water. As in Bulgaria, drums are beaten to stimulate the fire-walkers. Neither here nor in Fiji are the performers said to be entranced, like the Bulgarian Nistinares.[167] On the whole, the Kling rite (which the Klings, I am informed, also practise in the islands whither they are carried as coolies) so closely resembles the Fijian and the Tongan that one would explain the likeness by transmission, were the ceremony not almost as like the rite of the Hirpi. For the Tongan fire-ritual, the source is The Polynesian Society's Journal, vol. ii. No. 2. pp. 105-108. My attention was drawn to this by Mr. Laing, writing from New Zealand. The article is by Miss Tenira Henry, of Honolulu, a young lady of the island. The Council of the Society, not having seen the rite, 'do not guarantee the truth of the story, but willingly publish it for the sake of the incantation.' Miss Henry begins with a description of the ti-plant (Dracæna terminalis), which 'requires to be well baked before being eaten.' She proceeds thus:

'The ti-ovens are frequently thirty feet in diameter, and the large stones, heaped upon small logs of wood, take about twenty-four hours to get properly heated. Then they are flattened down, by means of long green poles, and the trunks of a few banana-trees are stripped up and strewn over them to cause steam. The ti-roots are then thrown in whole, accompanied by short pieces of apé-root (Arum costatum), that are not quite so thick as the ti, but grow to the length of six feet and more. The oven is then covered over with large leaves and soil, and left so for about three days, when the ti and the apé are taken out well cooked, and of a rich, light-brown colour. The apé prevents the ti from getting too dry in the oven.

'There is a strange ceremony connected with the Uum Ti (or ti-oven), that used to be practised by the heathen priests at Raiatea, but can now be performed by only two individuals (Tupua and Taero), both descendants of priests. This ceremony consisted in causing people to walk in procession through the hot oven when flattened down, before anything had been placed in it, and without any preparation whatever, bare-footed or shod, and on their emergence not even smelling of fire. The manner of doing this was told by Tupua, who heads the procession in the picture, to Monsieur Morné, Lieutenant de Vaisseau, who also took the photograph[168] of it, about two years ago, at Uturoa, Raiatea, which, being on bad

---

[167] Home, the medium, was, or affected to be, entranced in his fire tricks, as was Bernadette, at Lourdes, in the Miracle du Cierge.

[168] The photograph referred to is evidently taken from a sketch by hand, and is not therefore a photograph from life.—EDITOR. The original photograph was hereon sent to the editor and acknowledged by him.—A. L.

paper, was copied off by Mr. Barnfield, of Honolulu. All the white residents of the place, as well as the French officers, were present to see the ceremony, which is rarely performed nowadays.

'No one has yet been able to solve the mystery of this surprising feat, but it is to be hoped that scientists will endeavour to do so while those men who practise it still live.

Tupua's Incantation used in Walking Over the Uum-Ti.— Translation

'Hold the leaves of the ti-plant before picking them, and say: "O hosts of gods! awake, arise! You and I are going to the ti-oven to-morrow."

'If they float in the air, they are gods, but if their feet touch the ground they are human beings. Then break the ti-leaves off and look towards the direction of the oven, and say: "O hosts of gods! go to-night, and to-morrow you and I shall go." Then wrap the ti-leaves up in han (Hibiscus) leaves, and put them to sleep in the marae, where they must remain until morning, and say in leaving:

"'Arise! awake! O hosts of gods! Let your feet take you to the ti-oven; fresh water and salt water come also. Let the dark earth-worm and the light earth-worm go to the oven. Let the redness and the shades of fire all go. You will go; you will go to-night, and to-morrow it will be you and I; we shall go to the Uum-Ti." (This is for the night.)

'When the ti-leaves are brought away, they must be tied up in a wand and carried straight to the oven, and opened when all are ready to pass through; then hold the wand forward and say:

"'O men (spirits) who heated the oven! let it die out! O dark earth-worms! O light earthworms! fresh water and salt water, heat of the oven and redness of the oven, hold up the footsteps of the walkers, and fan the heat of the bed. O cold beings, let us lie in the midst of the oven! O Great-Woman-who-set-fire-to-the-skies! hold the fan, and let us go into the oven for a little while!" Then, when all are ready to walk in, we say:

> "Holder of the first footstep!
> Holder of the second footstep!
> Holder of the third footstep!
> Holder of the fourth footstep!
> Holder of the fifth footstep!
> Holder of the sixth footstep!
> Holder of the seventh footstep!
> Holder of the eighth footstep!
> Holder of the ninth footstep!
> Holder of the tenth footstep!
> "O Great-Woman-who-set-fire-to-the-skies! all is covered!"

107

'Then everybody walks through without hurt, into the middle and around the oven, following the leader, with the wand beating from side to side.

'The Great-Woman-who-set-fire-to-the-skies was a high-born woman in olden times, who made herself respected by the oppressive men when they placed women under so many restrictions. She is said to have had the lightning at her command, and struck men with it when they encroached on her rights.

'All the above is expressed in old Tahitian, and when quickly spoken is not easily understood by the modern listener. Many of the words, though found in the dictionary, are now obsolete, and the arrangement of others is changed. Oe and tana are never used now in place of the plural outou and tatou; but in old folk-lore it is the classical style of addressing the gods in the collective sense. Tahutahu means sorcery, and also to kindle a fire.'

* * * * *

So far Miss Henry, on this occasion, and the archaic nature of the hymn, with the reference to a mythical leader of the revolt of women, deserves the attention of anthropologists, apart from the singular character of the rite described. In the third number of the Journal (vol. ii.) the following editorial note is published:

'Miss Tenira Henry authorises us to say that her sister and her sister's little child were some of those who joined in the Uum-Ti ceremony referred to in vol. ii. p. 108, and in the preceding note, and actually walked over the red-hot stones. The illustration of the performance given in the last number of the Journal, it appears, is actually from a photograph taken by Lieutenant Morné, the original of which Miss Henry has sent us for inspection.—EDITOR.'

Corroborative Evidence

The following corroborative account is given in the Journal, from a source vaguely described as 'a pamphlet published in San Francisco, by Mr. Hastwell:'

'The natives of Raiatea have some performances so entirely out of the ordinary course of events as to institute (sic) inquiry relative to a proper solution.

'On September 20, 1885, I witnessed the wonderful, and to me inexplicable, performance of passing through the "fiery furnace."

'The furnace that I saw was an excavation of three or four feet in the ground, in a circular form (sloping upwards), and about thirty feet across. The excavation was filled with logs and wood, and then covered with large stones. A fire was built underneath, and kept burning for a day. When I witnessed it, on the second day, the flames were pouring up through the interstices of the rocks, which were heated to a red and white heat. When everything was in readiness, and the furnace still pouring out its intense heat, the natives marched up with bare feet to the edge of the furnace, where they halted for a moment, and after a few passes of the wand made of the branches of the ti-plant by the leader, who repeated a few words in the native language, they stepped down on the rocks and walked leisurely across to the other side, stepping from stone to stone. This was repeated five times, without any preparation whatever on their feet, and without injury or discomfort from the heated stones. There was not even the smell of fire on their garments.'

* * * * *

Mr. N. J. Tone, in the same periodical (ii. 3,193), says that he arrived just too late to see the same rite at Bukit Mestajam, in Province Wellesley, Straits Settlements; he did see the pit and the fire, and examined the naked feet, quite uninjured, of the performers. He publishes an extract to this effect from his diary. The performers, I believe, were Klings. Nothing is said to indicate any condition of trance, or other abnormal state, in the fire-walkers.

The Fire-walk in Trinidad.

Mr. Henry E. St. Clair, writing on September 14. 1896, says: 'In Trinidad, British West Indies, the rite is performed annually about this time of the year among the Indian coolie immigrants resident in the small village of Peru, a mile or so from Port of Spain. I have personally witnessed the passing, and the description given by Mr. Ponder tallies with what I saw, except that, so far as I can remember, the number of those who took part in the rite was greater than six. In addition, there is this circumstance, which was not mentioned by that gentleman: each of the "passers" carried one or two lemons, which they dropped into the fire as they went along. These lemons were afterwards eagerly scrambled for by the bystanders, who, so far as I can recollect, attributed a healing influence to them.'

Bulgarian Fire-walk

As to the Bulgarian rite, Dr. Schischmanof writes to me:

'I am sure the observance will surprise you; I am even afraid that you will think it rather fantastic, but you may rely on my information. The danse de feu was described long ago in a Bulgarian periodical by one of our best known writers. What you are about to read only confirms his account. What I send you is from the Recueil de Folk Lore, de Littérature et de Science (vol. vi. p. 224), edited, with my aid and that of my colleague, Mastov, by the Minister of Public Instruction. How will you explain these hauts faits de l'extase religieuse? I cannot imagine! For my part, I think of the self-mutilations and tortures of Dervishes and Fakirs, and wonder if we have not here something analogous.'

The article in the Bulgarian serial is called 'The Nistinares.' The word is not Bulgarian; possibly it is Romaic.

The scene is in certain villages in Turkey, on the Bulgarian frontier, and not far from the town of Bourgas, on the Euxine, in the department of Lozen Grad. The ministrants (Nistinares) have the gift of fire-walking as a hereditary talent; they are specially just, and the gift is attributed as to a god in Fiji, in Bulgaria to St. Constantine and St. Helena.

'These just ones feel a desire to dance in the flames during the month of May; they are filled at the same time with some unknown force, which enables them to predict the future. The best Nistinare is he who can dance longest in the live flame, and utter the most truthful prophecies.'

The Nistinares may be of either sex.

On May 1 the Nistinares hold a kind of religious festival at the house of one of their number. Salutations are exchanged, and presents of food and raki are made to the chief Nistinare. The holy icones of saints are wreathed with flowers, and perfumed with incense. Arrangements are made for purifying the holy wells and springs.

On May 21, the day of St. Helena and St. Constantine, the parish priest says Mass in the grey of dawn. At sunrise all the village meets in festal array; the youngest Nistinare brings from the church the icones of the two saints, and drums are carried behind them in procession. They reach the sacred well in the wood, which the priest blesses. This is parallel to the priestly benediction on 'Fountain Sunday' of the well beneath the Fairy Tree at Domremy,

110

where Jeanne d'Arc was accused of meeting the Good Ladies.[169] Everyone drinks of the water, and there is a sacrifice of rams, ewes, and oxen. A festival follows, as was the use of Domremy in the days of the Maid; then all return to the village. The holy drum, which hangs all the year before St. Helena in the church, is played upon. A mock combat between the icones which have visited the various holy wells is held.

Meanwhile, in each village, pyres of dry wood, amounting to thirty, fifty, or even a hundred cartloads, have been piled up. The wood is set on fire before the procession goes forth to the hallowing of the fountains. On returning, the crowd dances a horo (round dance) about the glowing logs. Heaps of embers (Pineus acervus) are made, and water is thrown on the ground. The musicians play the tune called 'L'Air Nistinar.' A Nistinare breaks through the dance, turns blue, trembles like a leaf, and glares wildly with his eyes. The dance ends, and everybody goes to the best point of view. Then the wildest Nistinare seizes the icon, turns it to the crowd, and with naked feet climbs the pyre of glowing embers. The music plays, and the Nistinare dances to the tune in the fire. If he is so disposed he utters prophecies. He dances till his face resumes its ordinary expression; then he begins to feel the burning; he leaves the pyre, and places his feet in the mud made by the libations of water already described. The second Nistinare then dances in the fire, and so on. The predictions apply to villages and persons; sometimes sinners are denounced, or repairs of the church are demanded in this queer parish council. All through the month of May the Nistinares call out for fire when they hear the Nistinare music playing. They are very temperate men and women. Except in May they do not clamour for fire, and cannot dance in it.

In this remarkable case the alleged gift is hereditary, is of saintly origin, and is only exercised when the Nistinare is excited, and (apparently) entranced by music and the dance, as is the manner also of medicine-men among savages. The rite, with its sacrifices of sheep and oxen, is manifestly of heathen origin. They 'pass through the fire' to St. Constantine, but the observance must be far older than Bulgarian Christianity. The report says nothing as to the state of the feet of the Nistinares after the fire-dance. Medical inspection is desirable, and the photographic camera should be used to catch a picture of the wild scene. My account is abridged from the French version of the Bulgarian report sent by Dr. Schischmanof.

---

[169] Procès, Quicherat, ii. 396, 397

Since these lines were written the kindness of Mr. Tawney, librarian at the India Office, has added to my stock of examples. Thus, Mr. Stokes printed in the Indian Antiquary (ii. p. 190) notes of evidence taken at an inquest on a boy of fourteen, who fell during the fire-walk, was burned, and died on that day. The rite had been forbidden, but was secretly practised in the village of Periyângridi. The fire-pit was 27 feet long by 7½ feet broad and a span in depth. Thirteen persons walked through the hot wood embers, which, in Mr. Stokes's opinion (who did not see the performance), 'would hardly injure the tough skin of the sole of a labourer's foot,' yet killed a boy. The treading was usually done by men under vows, perhaps vows made during illness. One, at least, walked 'because it is my duty as Pûjâri.' Another says, 'I got down into the fire at the east end, meditating on Draupatî, walked through to the west, and up the bank.' Draupatî is a goddess, wife of the Pândavas. Mr. Stokes reports that, according to the incredulous, experienced fire-walkers smear their feet with oil of the green frog. No report is made as to the condition of their feet when they emerge from the fire.

Another case occurs in Oppert's work, The Original Inhabitants of India (p. 480). As usual, a pit is dug, filled with faggots. When these have burned down 'a little,' and 'while the heat is still unbearable in the neighbourhood of the ditch, those persons who have made the vow . . . walk . . . on the embers in the pit, without doing themselves as a rule much harm.'

Again, in a case where butter is poured over the embers to make a blaze, 'one of the tribal priests, in a state of religious afflatus, walks through the fire. It is said that the sacred fire is harmless, but some admit that a certain preservative ointment is used by the performers.' A chant used at Mirzapur (as in Fiji) is cited.[170]

In these examples the statements are rather vague. No evidence is adduced as to the actual effect of the fire on the feet of the ministrants. We hear casually of ointments which protect the feet, and of the thickness of the skins of the fire-walkers, and of the unapproachable heat, but we have nothing exact, no trace of scientific precision. The Government 'puts down,' but does not really investigate the rite.

---

[170] ntroduction to Popular Religion and Folk-Lore in Northern India, by W. Crookes, B.A., p. 10.

I now very briefly, and 'under all reserves,' allude to the only modern parallel in our country with which I am acquainted. We have seen that Iamblichus includes insensibility to fire among the privileges of Græco-Egyptian 'mediums.'[171] The same gift was claimed by Daniel Dunglas Home, the notorious American spiritualist. I am well aware that as Eusapia Paladino was detected in giving a false impression that her hands were held by her neighbours in the dark, therefore, when Mr. Crookes asserts that he saw Home handle fire in the light, his testimony on this point can have no weight with a logical public. Consequently it is not as evidence to the fact that I cite Mr. Crookes, but for another purpose. Mr. Crookes's remarks I heard, and I can produce plenty of living witnesses to the same experiences with D. D. Home:

'I several times saw the fire test, both at my own and at other houses. On one occasion he called me to him when he went to the fire, and told me to watch carefully. He certainly put his hand in the grate and handled the red-hot coals in a manner which would have been impossible for me to have imitated without being severely burnt. I once saw him go to a bright wood fire, and, taking a large piece of red-hot charcoal, put it in the hollow of one hand, and, covering it with the other, blow into the extempore furnace till the coal was white hot, and the flames licked round his fingers. No sign of burning could be seen then or afterwards on his hands.'

On these occasions Home was, or was understood to be, 'entranced,' like the Bulgarian Nistinares. Among other phenomena, the white handkerchief on which Home laid a red-hot coal was not scorched, nor, on analysis, did it show any signs of chemical preparation. Home could also (like the Fijians) communicate his alleged immunity to others present; for example, to Mr. S. C. Hall. But it burned and marked a man I know. Home, entranced, and handling a red-hot coal, passed it to a gentleman of my acquaintance, whose hand still bears the scar of the scorching endured in 1867. Immunity was not always secured by experimenters.

I only mention these circumstances because Mr. Crookes has stated that he knows no chemical preparation which would avert the ordinary action of heat. Mr. Clodd (on the authority of Sir B. W. Richardson) has suggested diluted sulphuric acid (so familiar to Klings, Hirpi, Tongans, and Fijians). But Mr. Clodd produced no

---

[171] Iamblichus, De Myst. iii. 4.

examples of successful or unsuccessful experiment.[172]   The nescience of Mr. Crookes may be taken to cover these valuable properties of diluted sulphuric acid, unless Mr. Clodd succeeds in an experiment which, if made on his own person, I would very willingly witness.

Merely for completeness, I mention Dr. Dozous's statement,[173] that he timed by his watch Bernadette, the seer of Lourdes, while, for fifteen minutes, she, in an ecstatic condition, held her hands in the flame of a candle. He then examined her hands, which were not scorched or in any way affected by the fire. This is called, at Lourdes, the Miracle du Cierge.

Here ends my list of examples, in modern and ancient times, of a rite which deserves, though it probably will not receive, the attention of science. The widely diffused religious character of the performance will, perhaps, be admitted as demonstrated. As to the method by which the results are attained, whether by a chemical preparation, or by the influence of a certain mental condition, or by thickness of skin, or whether all the witnesses fable with a singular unanimity (shared by photographic cameras), I am unable even to guess. On May 21, in Bulgaria, a scientific observer might come to a conclusion. At present I think it possible that the Jewish 'Passing through the Fire' may have been a harmless rite.

Conclusion as to Fire-walk

In all these cases, and others as to which I have first-hand evidence, there are decided parallels to the Rite of the Hirpi, and to Biblical and ecclesiastical miracles. The savage examples are rites, and appear intended to secure good results in food supplies (Fiji), or general well-being, perhaps by expiation for sins, as in the Attic Thargelia. The Bulgarian rite also aims at propitiating general good luck.

Psychical Research

But how is the Fire-walk done? That remains a mystery, and perhaps no philologist, folk-lorist, anthropologist, or physiologist, has seriously asked the question. The medicamentum of Varro, the

---

[172] Folk-Lore, September 1895.
[173] Quoted by Dr. Boissarie in his book, Lourdes, p. 49, from a book by Dr. Dozous, now rare. Thanks to information from Dr. Boissarie, I have procured the book by Dr. Dozous, an eye-witness of the miracle, and have verified the quotation.

green frog fat of India, the diluted sulphuric acid of Mr. Clodd, are guesses in the air, and Mr. Clodd has made no experiment. The possibility of plunging the hand, unhurt, in molten metal, is easily accounted for, and is not to the point. In this difficulty Psychical Research registers, and no more, the well-attested performances of D. D. Home (entranced, like the Nistinares); the well observed and timed Miracle du Cierge at Lourdes—Bernadette being in an ecstatic condition; the Biblical story of Shadrach, Meshach, and Abednego in the fiery furnace; the researches of Iamblichus; the case of Madame Shchapoff, carefully reported,[174] and other examples. There is no harm in collecting examples, and the question remains, are all those rites, from those of Virgil's Hirpi to Bulgaria of to-day, based on some actual but obscure and scientifically neglected fact in nature? At all events, for the Soranus-Feronia rite philology only supplies her competing etymologies, folk-lore her modern rural parallels, anthropology her savage examples, psychical research her 'cases' at first-hand. Anthropology had neglected the collection of these, perhaps because the Fire-walk is 'impossible.'

---

[174] Predvestniki spiritizma za posleanie 250 lyet. A. M. Aksakoff, St. Petersburg, 1895. See Mr. Leaf's review, Proceedings S. P. R. xii. 329.

THE ORIGIN OF DEATH

Yama

This excursus on 'The Fire-walk' has been introduced, as an occasion arose, less because of controversy about a neglected theme than for the purpose of giving something positive in a controversial treatise. For the same reason I take advantage of Mr. Max Müller's remarks on Yama, 'the first who died,' to offer a set of notes on myths of the Origin of Death. Yama, in our author's opinion, is 'the setting sun' (i. 45; ii. 563). Agni (Fire) is 'the first who was born;' as the other twin, Yama, he was also the first who died (ii. 568). As 'the setting sun he was the first instance of death.' Kuhn and others, judging from a passage in the Atharva Veda (xviii. 3, 13), have, however, inferred that Yama 'was really a human being and the first of mortals.' He is described in the Atharva as 'the gatherer of men, who died the first of mortals, who went forward the first to that world.' In the Atharva we read of 'reverence to Yama, to Death, who first approached the precipice, finding out the path for many.' 'The myth of Yama is perfectly intelligible, if we trace its roots back to the sun of evening' (ii. 573). Mr. Max Müller then proposes on this head 'to consult the traditions of real Naturvölker' (savages). The Harvey Islanders speak of dying as 'following the sun's track.' The Maoris talk of 'going down with the sun' (ii. 574). No more is said here about savage myths of 'the first who died.' I therefore offer some additions to the two instances in which savages use a poetical phrase connecting the sun's decline with man's death.

The Origin of Death

Civilised man in a scientific age would never invent a myth to account for 'God's great ordinance of death.' He regards it as a fact, obvious and necessarily universal; but his own children have not attained to his belief in death. The certainty and universality of death do not enter into the thoughts of our little ones.

> For in the thought of immortality
> Do children play about the flowery meads.

Now, there are still many childlike tribes of men who practically disbelieve in death. To them death is always a surprise and an accident—an unnecessary, irrelevant intrusion on the living world. 'Natural deaths are by many tribes regarded as supernatural,' says Dr. Tylor. These tribes have no conception of

116

death as the inevitable, eventual obstruction and cessation of the powers of the bodily machine; the stopping of the pulses and processes of life by violence or decay or disease. To persons who regard Death thus, his intrusion into the world (for Death, of course, is thought to be a person) stands in great need of explanation. That explanation, as usual, is given in myths.

Death, regarded as Unnatural

But before studying these widely different myths, let us first establish the fact that death really is regarded as something non-natural and intrusive. The modern savage readily believes in and accounts in a scientific way for violent deaths. The spear or club breaks or crushes a hole in a man, and his soul flies out. But the deaths he disbelieves in are natural deaths. These he is obliged to explain as produced by some supernatural cause, generally the action of malevolent spirits impelled by witches. Thus the savage holds that, violence apart and the action of witches apart, man would even now be immortal. 'There are rude races of Australia and South America,' writes Dr. Tylor,[175] 'whose intense belief in witchcraft has led them to declare that if men were never bewitched, and never killed by violence, they would never die at all. Like the Australians, the Africans will inquire of their dead "what sorcerer slew them by his wicked arts."' 'The natives,' says Sir George Grey, speaking of the Australians, 'do not believe that there is such a thing as death from natural causes.' On the death of an Australian native from disease, a kind of magical coroner's inquest is held by the conjurers of the tribe, and the direction in which the wizard lives who slew the dead man is ascertained by the movements of worms and insects. The process is described at full length by Mr. Brough Smyth in his Aborigines of Victoria (i. 98-102). Turning from Australia to Hindustan, we find that the Puwarrees (according to Heber's narrative) attribute all natural deaths to a supernatural cause—namely, witchcraft. That is, the Puwarrees do not yet believe in the universality and necessity of Death. He is an intruder brought by magic arts into our living world. Again, in his Ethnology of Bengal (pp. 199, 200), Dalton tells us that the Hos (an aboriginal non-Aryan race) are of the same opinion as the Puwarrees. 'They hold that all disease in men or animals is attributable to one of two causes: the wrath of some evil spirit or the spell of some witch or sorcerer. These superstitions are common to all classes of the

---

[175] Prim. Cult. i. 138.

population of this province.' In the New Hebrides disease and death are caused, as Mr. Codrington found, by tamates, or ghosts.[176] In New Caledonia, according to Erskine, death is the result of witchcraft practised by members of a hostile tribe, for who would be so wicked as to bewitch his fellow-tribesman? The Andaman Islanders attribute all natural deaths to the supernatural influence of e rem chaugala, or to jurn-win, two spirits of the jungle and the sea. The death is avenged by the nearest relation of the deceased, who shoots arrows at the invisible enemy. The negroes of Central Africa entertain precisely similar ideas about the non-naturalness of death. Mr. Duff Macdonald, in Africana, writes: 'Every man who dies what we call a natural death is really killed by witches.' It is a far cry from the Blantyre Mission in Africa to the Eskimo of the frozen North; but so uniform is human nature in the lower races that the Eskimo precisely agree, as far as theories of death go, with the Africans, the aborigines of India, the Andaman Islanders, the Australians, and the rest. Dr. Rink[177] found that 'sickness or death coming about in an accidental manner was always attributed to witchcraft, and it remains a question whether death on the whole was not originally accounted for as resulting from magic.' Père Paul le Jeune, writing from Quebec in 1637, says of the Red Men: 'Je n'en voy mourir quasi aucun, qui ne pense estre ensorcelé.'[178] It is needless to show how these ideas survived into civilisation. Bishop Jewell, denouncing witches before Queen Elizabeth, was, so far, mentally on a level with the Eskimo and the Australian. The familiar and voluminous records of trials for witchcraft, whether at Salem or at Edinburgh, prove that all abnormal and unwonted deaths and diseases, in animals or in men, were explained by our ancestors as the results of supernatural mischief.

It has been made plain (and the proof might be enlarged to any extent) that the savage does not regard death as 'God's great ordinance,' universal and inevitable and natural. But, being curious and inquisitive, he cannot help asking himself, 'How did this terrible invader first enter a world where he now appears so often?' This is, properly speaking, a scientific question; but the savage answers it, not by collecting facts and generalising from them, but by inventing a myth. That is his invariable habit. Does he want to know why this tree has red berries, why that animal has brown stripes, why this bird utters its peculiar cry, where fire came from, why a constellation is grouped in one way or another, why his race

---

[176] Journal of Anthrop. Institute, x. iii.
[177] Tales and Traditions of the Eskimo, p. 42.
[178] Relations, 1637, p. 49.

of men differs from the whites—in all these, and in all other intellectual perplexities, the savage invents a story to solve the problem. Stories about the Origin of Death are, therefore, among the commonest fruits of the savage imagination. As those legends have been produced to meet the same want by persons in a very similar mental condition, it inevitably follows that they all resemble each other with considerable closeness. We need not conclude that all the myths we are about to examine came from a single original source, or were handed about—with flint arrow-heads, seeds, shells, beads, and weapons—in the course of savage commerce. Borrowing of this sort may—or, rather, must—explain many difficulties as to the diffusion of some myths. But the myths with which we are concerned now, the myths of the Origin of Death, might easily have been separately developed by simple and ignorant men seeking to discover an answer to the same problem.

Why Men are Mortal

The myths of the Origin of Death fall into a few categories. In many legends of the lower races men are said to have become subject to mortality because they infringed some mystic prohibition or taboo of the sort which is common among untutored peoples. The apparently untrammelled Polynesian, or Australian, or African, is really the slave of countless traditions, which forbid him to eat this object or to touch that, or to speak to such and such a person, or to utter this or that word. Races in this curious state of ceremonial subjection often account for death as the punishment imposed for breaking some taboo. In other cases, death is said to have been caused by a sin of omission, not of commission. People who have a complicated and minute ritual (like so many of the lower races) persuade themselves that Death burst on the world when some passage of the ritual was first omitted, or when some custom was first infringed. Yet again, Death is fabled to have first claimed us for his victims in consequence of the erroneous delivery of a favourable message from some powerful supernatural being, or because of the failure of some enterprise which would have resulted in the overthrow of Death, or by virtue of a pact or covenant between Death and the gods. Thus it will be seen that death is often (though by no means invariably) the penalty of infringing a command, or of indulging in a culpable curiosity. But there are cases, as we shall see, in which death, as a tolerably general law, follows on a mere accident. Some one is accidentally killed, and this 'gives Death a lead' (as they say in the hunting-field) over the fence which had hitherto severed him from the world of living men. It is to be observed in this connection that the first of men who died is usually regarded as the discoverer of a hitherto 'unknown country,' the land beyond the grave, to which all future men must follow him. Bin dir Woor, among the Australians, was the first man who suffered death, and he (like Yama in the Vedic myth) became the Columbus of the new world of the dead.

Savage Death-Myths

Let us now examine in detail a few of the savage stories of the Origin of Death. That told by the Australians may be regarded with suspicion, as a refraction from a careless hearing of the narrative in Genesis. The legend printed by Mr. Brough Smyth[179] was told to Mr. Bulwer by 'a black fellow far from sharp,' and this black fellow may conceivably have distorted what his tribe had heard from a missionary. This sort of refraction is not uncommon, and we must always guard ourselves against being deceived by a savage corruption of a Biblical narrative. Here is the myth, such as it is:— 'The first created man and woman were told' (by whom we do not learn) 'not to go near a certain tree in which a bat lived. The bat was not to be disturbed. One day, however, the woman was gathering firewood, and she went near the tree. The bat flew away, and after that came Death.' More evidently genuine is the following legend of how Death 'got a lead' into the Australian world. 'The child of the first man was wounded. If his parents could heal him, Death would never enter the world. They failed. Death came.' The wound in this legend was inflicted by a supernatural being. Here Death acts on the principle ce n'est que le premier pas qui coûte, and the premier pas was made easy for him. We may continue to examine the stories which account for death as the result of breaking a taboo. The Ningphos of Bengal say they were originally immortal.[180] They were forbidden to bathe in a certain pool of water. Some one, greatly daring, bathed, and ever since Ningphos have been subject to death. The infringement, not of a taboo, but of a custom, caused death in one of the many Melanesian myths on this subject. Men and women had been practically deathless because they cast their old skins at certain intervals; but a grandmother had a favourite grandchild who failed to recognise her when she appeared as a young woman in her new skin. With fatal good-nature the

---

[179] Abor. of Victoria, i. 429.
[180] Dalton, op. cit.

grandmother put on her old skin again, and instantly men lost the art of skin-shifting, and Death finally seized them.[181]

The Greek Myth

The Greek myth of the Origin of Death is the most important of those which turn on the breaking of a prohibition. The story has unfortunately become greatly confused in the various poetical forms which have reached us. As far as can be ascertained, death was regarded in one early Greek myth as the punishment of indulgence in forbidden curiosity. Men appear to have been free from death before the quarrel between Zeus and Prometheus. In consequence of this quarrel Hephæstus fashioned a woman out of earth and water, and gave her to Epimetheus, the brother of the Titan. Prometheus had forbidden his brother to accept any gift from the gods, but the bride was welcomed nevertheless. She brought her tabooed coffer: this was opened; and men—who, according to Hesiod, had hitherto lived exempt from 'maladies that bring down Fate'—were overwhelmed with the 'diseases that stalk abroad by night and day.' Now, in Hesiod (Works and Days, 70-100) there is nothing said about unholy curiosity. Pandora simply opened her casket and scattered its fatal contents. But Philodemus assures us that, according to a variant of the myth, it was Epimetheus who opened the forbidden coffer, whence came Death.

Leaving the myths which turn on the breaking of a taboo, and reserving for consideration the New Zealand story, in which the Origin of Death is the neglect of a ritual process, let us look at some African myths of the Origin of Death. It is to be observed that in these (as in all the myths of the most backward races) many of the characters are not gods, but animals.

The Bushman story lacks the beginning. The mother of the little Hare was lying dead, but we do not know how she came to die. The Moon then struck the little Hare on the lip, cutting it open, and saying, 'Cry loudly, for your mother will not return, as I do, but is quite dead.' In another version the Moon promises that the old Hare shall return to life, but the little Hare is sceptical, and is hit in the mouth as before. The Hottentot myth makes the Moon send the Hare to men with the message that they will revive as he (the Moon) does. But the Hare 'loses his memory as he runs' (to quote the French proverb, which may be based on a form of this very tale), and the messenger brings the tidings that men shall surely die and

---

[181] Codrington, Journal Anthrop. Institute, x. iii. For America, compare Relations de la Nouvelle France, 1674, p. 13.

121

never revive. The angry Moon then burns a hole in the Hare's mouth. In yet another Hottentot version the Hare's failure to deliver the message correctly caused the death of the Moon's mother (Bleek, Bushman Folklore).[182] Compare Sir James Alexander's Expedition, ii. 250, where the Namaquas tell this tale. The Fijians say that the Moon wished men to die and be born again, like herself. The Rat said, 'No, let them die, like rats;' and they do.[183]

The Serpent

In this last variant we have death as the result of a failure or transgression. Among the more backward natives of South India (Lewin's Wild Races of South India) the serpent is concerned, in a suspicious way, with the Origin of Death. The following legend might so easily arise from a confused understanding of the Mohammedan or Biblical narrative that it is of little value for our purpose. At the same time, even if it is only an adaptation, it shows the characteristics of the adapting mind:—God had made the world, trees, and reptiles, and then set to work to make man out of clay. A serpent came and devoured the still inanimate clay images while God slept. The serpent still comes and bites us all, and the end is death. If God never slept, there would be no death. The snake carries us off while God is asleep. But the oddest part of this myth remains. Not being able always to keep awake, God made a dog to drive away the snake by barking. And that is why dogs always howl when men are at the point of death. Here we have our own rural superstition about howling dogs twisted into a South Indian myth of the Origin of Death. The introduction of Death by a pure accident recurs in a myth of Central Africa reported by Mr. Duff Macdonald. There was a time when the man blessed by Sancho Panza had not yet 'invented sleep.' A woman it was who came and offered to instruct two men in the still novel art of sleeping. 'She held the nostrils of one, and he never awoke at all,' and since then the art of dying has been facile.

---

[182] The connection between the Moon and the Hare is also found in Sanskrit, in Mexican, in some of the South Sea Islands, and in German and Buddhist folklore. Probably what we call 'the Man in the Moon' seemed very like a hare to various races, roused their curiosity, and provoked explanations in the shape of myths.
[183] Hahn, Tsuni-Goam, p. 150.

Dualistic Myths

A not unnatural theory of the Origin of Death is illustrated by a myth from Pentecost Island and a Red Indian myth. In the legends of very many races we find the attempt to account for the Origin of Death and Evil by a simple dualistic myth. There were two brothers who made things; one made things well, the other made them ill. In Pentecost Island it was Tagar who made things well, and he appointed that men should die for five days only, and live again. But the malevolent Suque caused men 'to die right out.'[184] The Red Indian legend of the same character is printed in the Annual Report of the Bureau of Ethnology (1879-80), p. 45. The younger of the Cin-au-av brothers, who were wolves, said, 'When a man dies, send him back in the morning and let all his friends rejoice.' 'Not so,' said the elder; 'the dead shall return no more.' So the younger brother slew the child of the elder, and this was the beginning of death.

Economic Myth

There is another and a very quaint myth of the Origin of Death in Banks Island. At first, in Banks Island, as elsewhere, men were immortal. The economical results were just what might have been expected. Property became concentrated in the hands of the few—that is, of the first generations—while all the younger people were practically paupers. To heal the disastrous social malady, Qat (the maker of things, who was more or less a spider) sent for Mate— that is, Death. Death lived near a volcanic crater of a mountain, where there is now a by-way into Hades—or Panoi, as the Melanesians call it. Death came, and went through the empty forms of a funeral feast for himself. Tangaro the Fool was sent to watch Mate, and to see by what way he returned to Hades, that men might avoid that path in future. Now when Mate fled to his own place, this great fool Tangaro noticed the path, but forgot which it was, and pointed it out to men under the impression that it was the road to the upper, not to the under, world. Ever since that day men have been constrained to follow Mate's path to Panoi and the dead.[185] Another myth is somewhat different, but, like this one, attributes death to the imbecility of Tangaro the Fool.

---

[184] Codrington, op. cit, p. 304.
[185] Codrington, op. cit.

123

Maui and Yama

The New Zealand myth of the Origin of Death is pretty well known, as Dr. Tylor has seen in it the remnants of a solar myth, and has given it a 'solar' explanation. It is an audacious thing to differ from so cautious and learned an anthropologist as Dr. Tylor, but I venture to give my reasons for dissenting in this case from the view of the author of Primitive Culture (i. 335). Maui is the great hero of Maori mythology. He was not precisely a god, still less was he one of the early elemental gods, yet we can scarcely regard him as a man. He rather answers to one of the race of Titans, and especially to Prometheus, the son of a Titan. Maui was prematurely born, and his mother thought the child would be no credit to her already numerous and promising family. She therefore (as native women too often did in the South-Sea Islands) tied him up in her long tresses and tossed him out to sea. The gales brought him back to shore: one of his grandparents carried him home, and he became much the most illustrious and successful of his household. So far Maui had the luck which so commonly attends the youngest and least-considered child in folklore and mythology. This feature in his myth may be a result of the very widespread custom of jüngsten Recht (Borough English), by which the youngest child is heir at least of the family hearth. Now, unluckily, at the baptism of Maui (for a pagan form of baptism is a Maori ceremony) his father omitted some of the Karakias, or ritual utterances proper to be used on such occasions. This was the fatal original mistake whence came man's liability to death, for hitherto men had been immortal. So far, what is there 'solar' about Maui? Who are the sun's brethren?—and Maui had many. How could the sun catch the sun in a snare, and beat him so as to make him lame? This was one of Maui's feats, for he meant to prevent the sun from running too fast through the sky. Maui brought fire, indeed, from the under-world, as Prometheus stole it from the upper-world; but many men and many beasts do as much as the myths of the world, and it is hard to see how the exploit gives Maui 'a solar character.' Maui invented barbs for hooks, and other appurtenances of early civilisation, with which the sun has no more to do than with patent safety-matches. His last feat was to attempt to secure human immortality for ever. There are various legends on this subject.

Maui Myths

Some say Maui noticed that the sun and moon rose again from their daily death, by virtue of a fountain in Hades (Hine-nui-te-po) where they bathed. Others say he wished to kill Hine-nui-te-po (conceived of as a woman) and to carry off her heart. Whatever the reason, Maui was to be swallowed up in the giant frame of Hades, or Night, and, if he escaped alive, Death would never have power over men. He made the desperate adventure, and would have succeeded but for the folly of one of the birds which accompanied him. This little bird, which sings at sunset, burst out laughing inopportunely, wakened Hine-nui-te-po, and she crushed to death Maui and all hopes of earthly immortality. Had he only come forth alive, men would have been deathless. Now, except that the bird which laughed sings at sunset, what is there 'solar' in all this? The sun does daily what Maui failed to do,[186] passes through darkness and death back into light and life. Not only does the sun daily succeed where Maui failed, but it was his observation of this fact which encouraged Maui to risk the adventure. If Maui were the sun, we should all be immortal, for Maui's ordeal is daily achieved by the sun. But Dr. Tylor says:[187] 'It is seldom that solar characteristics are more distinctly marked in the several details of a myth than they are here.' To us the characteristics seem to be precisely the reverse of solar. Throughout the cycle of Maui he is constantly set in direct opposition to the sun, and the very point of the final legend is that what the sun could do Maui could not. Literally the one common point between Maui and the sun is that the little bird, the tiwakawaka, which sings at the daily death of day, sang at the eternal death of Maui.

Without pausing to consider the Tongan myth of the Origin of Death, we may go on to investigate the legends of the Aryan races. According to the Satapatha Brahmana, Death was made, like the gods and other creatures, by a being named Prajapati. Now of Prajapati, half was mortal, half was immortal. With his mortal half he feared Death, and concealed himself from Death in earth and water. Death said to the gods, 'What hath become of him who created us?' They answered, 'Fearing thee, hath he entered the earth.' The gods and Prajapati now freed themselves from the dominion of Death by celebrating an enormous number of sacrifices. Death was chagrined by their escape from the 'nets and clubs' which he carries in the Aitareya Brahmana. 'As you have escaped me, so will men also escape,' he grumbled. The gods appeased him by the promise that, in the body, no man henceforth for ever should evade Death. 'Every one who is to become immortal shall do so by first parting with his body.'

[186] Bastian, Heilige Sage.
[187] Primitive Culture, i. 336.

Yama

Among the Aryans of India, as we have already seen, Death has a protomartyr, Tama, 'the first of men who reached the river, spying out a path for many.' In spying the path Yama corresponds to Tangaro the Fool, in the myth of the Solomon Islands. But Yama is not regarded as a maleficent being, like Tangaro. The Rig Veda (x. 14) speaks of him as 'King Yama, who departed to the mighty streams and sought out a road for many;' and again, the Atharva Veda names him 'the first of men who died, and the first who departed to the celestial world.' With him the Blessed Fathers dwell for ever in happiness. Mr. Max Müller, as we said, takes Yama to be 'a character suggested by the setting sun'—a claim which is also put forward, as we have seen, for the Maori hero Maui. It is Yama, according to the Rig Veda, who sends the birds—a pigeon is one of his messengers (compare the White Bird of the Oxenhams)—as warnings of approaching death. Among the Iranian race, Yima appears to have been the counterpart of the Vedic Yama. He is now King of the Blessed; originally he was the first of men over whom Death won his earliest victory.

Inferences

That Yama is mixed up with the sun, in the Rig Veda, seems certain enough. Most phenomena, most gods, shade into each other in the Vedic hymns. But it is plain that the conception of a 'first man who died' is as common to many races as it is natural. Death was regarded as unnatural, yet here it is among us. How did it come? By somebody dying first, and establishing a bad precedent. But need that somebody have been originally the sun, as Mr. Max Müller and Dr. Tylor think in the cases of Yama and Maui? This is a point on which we may remain in doubt, for death in itself was certain to challenge inquiry among savage philosophers, and to be explained by a human rather than by a solar myth. Human, too, rather than a result of 'disease of language' is, probably, the myth of the Fire-stealer.

The Stealing of Fire

The world-wide myth explaining how man first became possessed of fire—namely, by stealing it—might well serve as a touchstone of the philological and anthropological methods. To Mr. Max Müller the interest of the story will certainly consist in discovering connections between Greek and Sanskrit names of fire-gods and of fire bringing heroes. He will not compare the fire-myths of other races all over the world, nor will he even try to explain why—in almost all of these myths we find a thief of fire, a Fire-stealer. This does not seem satisfactory to the anthropologist, whose first curiosity is to know why fire is everywhere said to have been obtained for men by sly theft or 'flat burglary.' Of course it is obvious that a myth found in Australia and America cannot possibly be the result of disease of Aryan languages not spoken in those two continents. The myth of fire-stealing must necessarily have some other origin.

'Fire Totems'

Mr. Max Müller, after a treatise on Agni and other fire-gods, consecrates two pages to 'Fire Totems.' 'If we are assured that there are some dark points left, and that these might be illustrated and rendered more intelligible by what are called fire totems among the Red Indians of North America, let us have as much light as we can get' (ii. 804). Alas! I never heard of fire totems before. Probably some one has been writing about them, somewhere, unless we owe them to Mr. Max Müller's own researches. Of course, he cites no authority for his fire totems. 'The fire totem, we are told, would thus naturally have become the god of the Indians.' 'We are told'—where, and by whom? Not a hint is given on the subject, so we must leave the doctrine of fire totems to its mysterious discoverer. 'If others prefer to call Prometheus a fire totem, no one would object, if only it would help us to a better understanding of Prometheus' (ii. 810). Who are the 'others' who speak of a Greek 'culture-hero' by the impossibly fantastic name of 'a fire totem'?

Prometheus

Mr. Max Müller 'follows Kuhn' in his explanation of Prometheus, the Fire-stealer, but he does not follow him all the way. Kuhn tried to account for the myth that Prometheus stole fire, and Mr. Max Müller does not try.[188] Kuhn connects Prometheus with the Sanskrit pramantha, the stick used in producing fire by drilling a pointed into a flat piece of wood. The Greeks, of course, made Prometheus mean 'foresighted,' providens; but let it be granted that the Germans know better. Pramantha next is associated with the verb mathnami, 'to rub or grind;' and that, again, with Greek μανθανω, 'to learn.' We too talk of a student as a 'grinder,' by a

---

[188] Kuhn, Die Herabkunft der Feuers und der Göttertranks. Berlin, 1859.

coincidence. The root manth likewise means 'to rob;' and we can see in English how a fire-stick, a 'fire-rubber,' might become a 'fire-robber,' a stealer of fire. A somewhat similar confusion in old Aryan languages converted the fire-stick into a person, the thief of fire, Prometheus; while a Greek misunderstanding gave to Prometheus (pramantha, 'fire-stick') the meaning of 'foresighted,' with the word for prudent foresight, προμηθεια. This, roughly stated, is the view of Kuhn.[189] Mr. Max Müller concludes that Prometheus, the producer of fire, is also the fire-god, a representative of Agni, and necessarily 'of the inevitable Dawn'—'of Agni as the deus matutinus, a frequent character of the Vedic Agni, the Agni aushasa, or the daybreak' (ii. 813).

But Mr. Max Müller does not say one word about Prometheus as the Fire-stealer. Now, that he stole fire is of the essence of his myth; and this myth of the original procuring of fire by theft occurs all over the world. As Australian and American savages cannot conceivably have derived the myth of fire-stealing from the root manth and its double sense of stealing and rubbing, there must be some other explanation. But this fact could not occur to comparative mythologists who did not compare, probably did not even know, similar myths wherever found.

Savage Myths of Fire-stealing

In La Mythologie (pp. 185-195) I have put together a small collection of savage myths of the theft of fire.[190] Our text is the line of Hesiod (Theogony, 566), 'Prometheus stole the far-seen ray of unwearied fire in a hollow stalk of fennel.' The same stalk is still used in the Greek isles for carrying fire, as it was of old—whence no doubt this feature of the myth.[191] How did Prometheus steal fire? Some say from the altar of Zeus, others that he lit his rod at the sun.[192] The Australians have the same fable; fire was obtained by a black fellow who climbed by a rope to the sun. Again, in Australia fire was the possession of two women alone. A man induced them to turn their backs, and stole fire. A very curious version of the myth occurs in an excellent book by Mrs. Langloh Parker.[193] There

---

[189] Herabkunft, pp. 16, 24.
[190] Dupret, Paris, 1886. Translation by M. Parmentier.
[191] Pliny, Hist. Nat. xiii. 22. Bent. Cyclades.
[192] Servius ad Virg., Eclogue vi. 42.
[193] Australian Legendary Tales. Nutt: London, 1897. Mrs. Parker knows Australian dialects, and gives one story in the original. Her tribes live on the Narran River, in New South Wales.

was no fire when Rootoolgar, the crane, married Gooner, the kangaroo rat. Rootoolgar, idly rubbing two sticks together, discovered the art of fire-making. 'This we will keep secret,' they said, 'from all the tribes.' A fire-stick they carried about in their comebee. The tribes of the Bush discovered the secret, and the fire-stick was stolen by Reeargar, the hawk. We shall be told, of course, that the hawk is the lightning, or the Dawn. But in this savage Jungle Book all the characters are animals, and Reeargar is no more the Dawn than is the kangaroo rat. In savage myths animals, not men, play the leading rôles, and the fire-stealing bird or beast is found among many widely scattered races. In Normandy the wren is the fire-bringer.[194] A bird brings fire in the Andaman Isles.[195] Among the Ahts a fish owned fire; other beasts stole it. The raven hero of the Thlinkeets, Yehl, stole fire. Among the Cahrocs two old women possessed it, and it was stolen by the coyote. Are these theftuous birds and beasts to be explained as Fire-gods? Probably not. Will any philologist aver that in Cahroc, Thlinkeet. Australian, Andaman, and so forth, the word for 'rub' resembled the word for 'rob,' and so produced by 'a disease of language' the myth of the Fire-stealer?

Origin of the Myth of Fire-stealing

The myth arose from the nature of savage ideas, not from unconscious puns. Even in a race so civilised as the Homeric Greeks, to make fire was no easy task. Homer speaks of a man, in a lonely upland hut, who carefully keeps the embers alive, that he may not have to go far afield in search of the seed of fire.[196] Obviously he had no ready means of striking a light. Suppose, then, that an early savage loses his seed of fire. His nearest neighbours, far enough off, may be hostile. If he wants fire, as they will not give it, he must steal it, just as he must steal a wife. People in this condition would readily believe, like the Australian blacks, that the original discoverers or possessors of a secret so valuable as fire would not give it away, that others who wanted it would be obliged to get it by theft. In Greece, in a civilised race, this very natural old idea survives, though fire is not the possession of a crane, or of an old woman, but of the gods, and is stolen, not by a hawk or a coyote, but by Prometheus, the culture-hero and demiurge. Whether his name 'Foresighted' is a mistaken folk-etymology from the root manth, or

---

[194] Bosquet, La Normandie Merveilleuse. Paris, 1845.
[195] Journal Anthrop. Institute, November, 1884.
[196] Odyssey, v. 488-493.

not, we have, in the ancient inevitable idea, that the original patentees of fire would not willingly part with their treasure, the obvious origin of the myth of the Fire-stealer. And this theory does not leave the analogous savage myths of fire-stealing unexplained and out in the cold, as does the philological hypothesis.[197] In this last instance, as in others, the origin of a world-wide myth is found, not in a 'disease of language,' but in a form of thought still natural. If a foreign power wants what answers among us to the exclusive possession of fire, or wants the secret of its rival's new explosive, it has to steal it.

---

[197] References for savage myths of the Fire-stealer will be found—for the Ahts, in Sproat; for the tribes of the Pacific coast, in Bancroft; for Australians in Brough Smyth's Aborigines of Victoria.

CONCLUSION

Here ends this 'Gentle and Joyous Passage of Arms.' I showed, first, why anthropological students of mythology, finding the philological school occupying the ground, were obliged in England to challenge Mr. Max Müller. I then discoursed of some inconveniences attending his method in controversy. Next, I gave a practical example, the affair of Tuna and Daphne. This led to a comparison of the philological and the anthropological ways of treating the Daphne myth. The question of our allies then coming up, I stated my reasons for regarding Prof. Tiele 'rather as an ally than an adversary,' the reason being his own statement. Presently, I replied to Prof. Tiele's criticism of my treatment of the myth of Cronos. After a skirmish on Italian fields, I gave my reasons for disagreeing with Mr. Max Müller's view of Mannhardt's position. His theory of Demeter Erinnys was contrasted with that of Mr. Max Müller. Totemism occupied us next, and the views of Mr. Max Müller and Mr. J. G. Frazer were criticised. Then I defended anthropological and criticised philological evidence. Our method of universal comparison was next justified in the matter of Fetishism. The Riddle Theory of Mr. Max Müller was presently discussed. Then followed a review of our contending methods in the explanation of Artemis, of the Fire-walk, of Death Myths, and of the Fire-stealer. Thus a number of points in mythological interpretation have been tested on typical examples.

Much more might be said on a book of nearly 900 pages. Many points might be taken, much praise (were mine worth anything) might be given; but I have had but one object, to defend the method of anthropology from a running or dropping fire of criticism which breaks out in many points all along the line, through Contributions to the Science of Mythology. If my answer be desultory and wandering, remember the sporadic sharpshooting of the adversary! For adversary we must consider Mr. Max Müller, so long as we use different theories to different results. If I am right, if he is wrong, in our attempts to untie this old Gordian knot, he loses little indeed. That fame of his, the most steady and brilliant light of all which crown the brows of contemporary scholars, is the well-earned reward, not of mythological lore nor of cunning fence in controversy, but of wide learning and exquisitely luminous style.

I trust that I have imputed no unfairness, made no charge of conscious misrepresentation (to accidents of exposition we are all liable), have struck no foul blow, hazarded no discourteous phrase.

131

If I have done so, I am thereby, even more than in my smattering of unscholarly learning, an opponent more absolutely unworthy of the Right Hon. Professor than I would fain believe myself.

APPENDIX A

The Fire-walk in Spain

One study occasionally illustrates another. In examining the history of the Earl Marischal, who was exiled after the rising of 1715, I found, in a letter of a correspondent of d'Alembert, that the Earl met a form of the fire-walk in Spain. There then existed in the Peninsula a hereditary class of men who, by dint of 'charms' permitted by the Inquisition, could enter fire unharmed. The Earl Marischal said that he would believe in their powers if he were allowed first to light the fire, and then to look on. But the fire-walkers would not gratify him, as not knowing what kind of fire a heretic might kindle.

APPENDIX B

Mr. Macdonell on Vedic Mythology

Too late for use here came Vedic Mythology, from Grundriss der indo-arischen Philologie,[198] by Mr. A. Macdonell, the representative of the historic house of Lochgarry. This even a non-scholar can perceive to be a most careful and learned work. As to philological 'equations' between names of Greek and Vedic gods, Mr. Macdonell writes: 'Dyaus=Ζευς is the only one which can be said to be beyond the range of doubt.' As to the connection of Prometheus with Sanskrit Pramantha, he says: 'Προμηθευς has every appearance of being a purely Greek formation, while the Indian verb math, to twirl, is found compounded only with nis, never with pra, to express the art of producing fire by friction.' (See above, p. 194.) If Mr. Macdonell is right here, the Greek myth of the fire-stealer cannot have arisen from 'a disease of language.' But scholars must be left to reconcile this last typical example of their ceaseless differences in the matter of etymology of names.

---

[198] Trübner, Strasburg, 1897.

Lightning Source UK Ltd.
Milton Keynes UK
UKHW041017020720
365860UK00001B/32